WHISKY SOUR

WHISKY SOUR

George Pottinger

795061 |ŀ

Paul Harris Publishing

Edinburgh

First published in Great Britain 1979 by
Paul Harris Publishing
25 London Street
Edinburgh
Scotland

ISBN 0 904505 62 6

Photoset, printed and bound
in Great Britain by
REDWOOD BURN LIMITED
Trowbridge & Esher

'Glenmorangie, Glen Livet,
Hear the Holy Highland Chant:
Portree, Laphroaig and Talisker,
Glenfiddich and Glen Grant.'

Old Whisky Ballad

Prologue

'Advance Britannia. Long live the cause of freedom.'
Churchill's panegyric to mark the end of the war in Europe was
the last sound that Torquil McLeish, Fourteenth Laird of
McLeish, heard on the wireless. That was five days ago. He had
been in a coma ever since, and now he had gone to his long rest.
Alison McLeish, newly-widowed, drew the sheet over his mask-
like face. She went to close the curtains.

'Jessie, the Laird's away,' Alison called. Mrs Macleod had
served the McLeish family for many years since her husband
was killed at Loos in the First War. Latterly she had been
housekeeper, and only the Laird and his wife called her Jessie.
Now the two widows embraced, and while they wept, Jessie, as
the senior, gave silent comfort to her mistress.

'Come, Jessie.' Alison dried her tears. 'There's much to be
done. Tell Angus to lower the flag to half-mast, and he should
let them know in the village. I'll ring Mr Porteous.'

'Ay. I'll do that. This is a sad day for Skye. There'll be many
throughout the Island that'll mourn his passing.'

James Porteous, Solicitor and Notary Public at Portree,
looked after the affairs of the McLeish Estate. It was his largest
client. He undertook such legal transactions as became necessary, and since in wartime there was no grieve or Estate manager, he did the factoring as well. He was not unprepared for
the Laird's demise. He had already drafted the notice for *The
Times* and *The Scotsman*.

7

'At The Keep, Lower Borve, Isle of Skye, peacefully in his sixty-seventh year, Torquil McLeish, C.B., D.S.O., Fourteenth Laird of McLeish, only son of the late General Sir Charles Edward McLeish and Lady McLeish; Major-General (retired), late the Queen's Own Cameron Highlanders; His Majesty's Vice-Lieutenant for Inverness-shire; beloved husband of Alison and father of David and Charles Edward. Funeral Service at St Columba's, Lower Borve, at 2.30.p.m. on Friday 18th June, 1945, and thereafter at the McLeish burial ground.'

'My deepest sympathy, Alison,' the lawyer said. 'I'll miss him as a good friend and a great Scotsman. But we knew he was going. David will be the new Laird. Will he and his brother be back in time?'

'I know David will. I've sent him a telegram, and I'm going to ring Scottish Command to see if Charlie can be sent home.'

After only a short delay she was connected to the G.O.C.'s personal extension.

'Fergie, this is Alison McLeish.'

'It's good to hear you. Are you in Edinburgh?' Lieutenant-General Sir Fergus Callander had a premonition of unwelcome news, but he was a kindly man, and Alison was an old friend.

'Torquil's away.'

'I'm so sorry. You'll accept my heartfelt condolences.'

'Thank you, Fergie. He was content to see the war out. I think he gave up the struggle when he heard Winston, and he was so glad that Charlie had been spared. David too.'

'He'll still be a loss. He was a great man in the Regiment, and we all looked up to him.' Callander was thinking of the implications. 'There's a Company at Portree who'll provide the Guard of Honour. I'll ask the Navy at Aultbea to be represented. It won't be as formal as we'd have liked, but I'll see there's a good muster. What about your piper? Have you got someone for the pibroch?' Callander knew Torquil was the kind of man who would want to be played into the next world, to let them hear the sound of a Chief. 'Do you want me to speak to the Depot?'

'No. I'll ask Flora. She'll help, I know she will.' Flora Macleod was Chieftain of all the Macleods. Their hereditary pipers were schooled by the McCrimmons from Borroreg, the most celebrated of those who played the Great Music. 'But that's not what I meant to ask you. I want to get Charlie back.'

'Where is he?'

'Italy, with the Eighth Army. He was somewhere near Riccione when he last wrote.'

'That shouldn't be too difficult. We'll have him flown over. God bless, Alison, and if you'll take my advice, have a stiff dram tonight. That's what he would have prescribed.'

David McLeish, newly Fifteenth of McLeish, temporary Assistant Secretary at the Cabinet Office, looked at the telegram with mixed feelings. As a boy, he had never been close to his father, and once he had grown up the distance between them had lengthened. Rheumatic fever, caught after being drenched while stalking, had left a murmur in his heart and precluded an Army career. His father had made no effort to conceal his disappointment, or his scorn for the cerebral interests which his elder son had pursued at school, at Cambridge as an undergraduate and as a Research Fellow, and, since the outbreak of war, in the Civil Service. David's return journeys to The Keep had become rarer, and, since he could plead the difficulties of wartime travel, had almost ceased. Only his affections for his mother would occasionally turn his thoughts towards the family home.

On his last visit he had suffered when the General had challenged him to spend a day on the hill. David had declined, and his father, returning triumphant with a prime stag, had taunted him with his unwillingness, his disability, and more cruelly with his apprehension. His mother had intervened, only to earn a scowl and a muttered imprecation, and he had realised that the McLeish mystique with its emphasis on death and killing – first rival clansmen, then natives overseas, and more recently Boche (twice), while game was hunted incessantly – was not for him. He felt no remorse at deserting a tradition monotonously followed by McLeishes for many generations. Not for him the

9

glories and splendours of De Vigny's *vie militaire*. He had opted for the rational solution.

He had not considered the implications of inheriting the Estate. That, being an unsympathetic subject, was kept in the background. It could still wait for a day or two, until he returned to The Keep and heard the wily Porteous's account of his stewardship. Meanwhile, the summons could not have come at a worse time. An important mission was about to leave for Washington, and he had been told he might be included. This was not the moment to be away from Whitehall. He had also planned another attempt to entice Kirsty to dine with him. But he had no choice. He rang the travel branch. Fortunately his temporary rank entitled him to priority in booking a berth on the sleeper to Inverness.

Major Charles Edward McLeish, M.C., R.A., one of the many McLeishes still christened with overtly Jacobite names, was floating on his back in the Adriatic, with his toes in the ears of his Italian mistress.

Married to a rich Bolognese, Beatrice had come to Riccione to reopen and protect the family's seaside villa. Charlie found her fluency in his own tongue – she had an English mother – an added attraction. He did not have to rely on the troops' range of Italian phrases and suggestive gestures to equip her absent husband with a set of cuckold's horns. Beatrice, for her part, enjoyed liberation to the point of licence.

'That tickles, *tesoro*.' Charlie's reply was to push her under.

'Major McLeish, Sir.' The Battery Clerk was waving from the beach. 'It's the Adjutant, Sir. He says the C.O. wants to see you at once.'

'Tell him I'm engaged on local liaison.' Charlie cursed gently. Regimental Headquarters was a poor exchange for Beatrice's opulent charms, but he waded ashore.

'Charlie, I've got bad news for you.' The Colonel sounded gruff. 'Your father's died. I'm very sorry.'

'Thank you, Sir. I'm sorry you had the embarrassment of telling me,' Charlie replied automatically. At first he did not fully comprehend what had been said. After more than two years overseas, the memory of his father had become dimmer. But it was unbelievable that he had gone. He had seemed impervious to the passage of time, a permanent feature of the landscape – like The Keep itself, or Ben More, or the Prince Charles Edward Memorial at Glenfinnan. His mother's last letter had contained an undercurrent of warning, but there had been no reason to expect the final blow so soon.

'He had a good life, Charlie. Very distinguished career. Everyone admired him. You will have many happy memories.' The C.O., like his junior officer, had looked on death at first hand, but news of this kind from home seemed all the more painful.

'Good of you to say so. You're quite right.' His relationship with his father had been friendly, affectionate, respectful. He had followed the General's precepts without question. Most of them had been predictable, except when his father pronounced in favour of the Artillery for his son, instead of his own cherished Infantry Regiment. The day of the foot-soldier was over, he told Charlie. It had ended in the First War, which he had been lucky to survive. It had probably been finished when Captain Belford's guns destroyed the loyal troops at Culloden. In the face of such an unshakeable Jacobite precedent Charlie had not argued. He had gone to the Shop at Woolwich, instead of Sandhurst, and his belief in a comfortable order of things had received its first shock when his brother declined to witness his passing-out parade, the last, as it transpired, before the Second War brought such formalities to a hurried end.

David, angular, ascetic, caustic David, his much admired elder brother. Charlie had never shared his father's contempt for David's way of life, but when he spoke up for him he had met with a cold reproof. The General made clear it was none of his business; David said he wanted no help from a semi-literate younger brother who had taken the easy option of the King's Shilling; and Charlie was left baffled and hurt. He could understand his brother's nausea at reeking carcasses brought from the hill, or salmon lying on the stone slab for the General's in-

11

spection, but his sarcastic comments on life among the 'thicks and hicks', as he referred to those who held His Majesty's Commission, had been permanently wounding. Dumb soldiers had, however, had their uses in the last few years. Special train for Atkins. Not always so dumb, Charlie thought, particularly in the early stages when he had mastered the arcane mysteries of the artillery tables, logarithms, and the slide rule. Would his hard-won proficiency still have aroused David's disdain? Probably.

'You're flying home tomorrow. We've been speaking to the Americans at Cesenatico. Thanks to that party we gave, they're prepared to find a place for you on a plane to England. Leaves at 0600 hours, so you're to spend tonight with them. You'd better take your month's leave at the same time. There will be things to settle.'

'Very kind of you, Sir.' The furlough arrangements had been a source of grievance. Under the Python scheme those with two and a half years abroad became eligible for a month at home. Charlie was not at the top of the list, and the C.O.'s dispensation was generous.

Time to pack and hand over the Battery. There would be no chance to say goodbye to Beatrice, but that had its own advantages. Disengagement could be awkward, and he would be replaced in her affections, and elsewhere, long before he returned. Charlie had an occasional streak of the ruthlessness that was more evident in his father and brother. With a month's leave, he would be able to see Kirsty and demonstrate in person that his letters meant what they said.

Kirsty Shaw, First Officer, W.R.N.S., was more immediately affected by the General's death than either of his sons. Reading the notice in *The Times* during her coffee break at the Admiralty, she remembered how kind he had been to her. The daughter of a Writer to the Signet, as the more prosperous Edinburgh lawyers call themselves, she had met the Clan McLeish when on holiday in Skye with her uncle,

James Porteous. The General and his wife had taken a liking to her. He had asked her to fish and had taught her the elements of casting. She found a lonely, empty man, disappointed in his elder son, and little more than tolerant of Charlie. On later visits to The Keep she felt she was closer to the Laird than either of them, but she became more wary when she was asked to join the House party for the Skye Gathering, the event of the year in the Island's social calendar. There was a change in the way Alison McLeish regarded her. She was no longer seen as a boyish figure tying flies and throwing a line over the Laird's Pool. She was a possible daughter-in-law.

Scanning the obituary, Kirsty recalled the moment when it struck her that she was intended to be the châtelaine of the gaunt Highland fortress. They had come early from the river for tea, before a bath and changing for the Ball. She had sat at the General's feet. He was looking at his sons in the deep embrasure of the sitting-room, but it was her he addressed. A good life, Kirsty, he said. Civilised too. All anyone could want, if they were wise.

David's interest had manifested itself repeatedly. Since she had been posted to the Admiralty he had often asked her to dinner. He was a good host, charming, witty, with a keen eye for ridicule. He seldom spoke of his family, and then, except for his mother, with a distant scorn that she found chilling. That was the trouble. He was too like the chilled claret which he had once rejected so indignantly, saying that until the Goths finally sacked the West End his wine would be at the right temperature. There was something about his acid self-analysis that she found repellent. Recently she had done her best to discourage him, but the siege had not been lifted.

Charlie she had never regarded as anything but a younger brother, although he was a year older than she was. She remembered the vigorous, but still elegant way he had partnered her in the traditional country dances, and his hurried kiss after supper. Since he had gone overseas he had written to her with amazing regularity, strange, gauche letters whose contents were pregnant with all kinds of embarrassment for the future.

13

She would write to tell Mrs McLeish that she shared her sorrow. But she was relieved that duties in Whitehall gave her a reason for not meeting the brothers.

As he crossed the saddle a few miles west of Portree, David felt an involuntary stirring. He had to admit that this had always been the first sign that he was nearly home. A Uig farmer had given him a lift from the ferry at Kyleakin, but their conversation had dwindled, and the last half-hour had been almost completely silent. There had been little maintenance done on the single-track road. Rushes and weeds thrust impertinently through the surface and the passing-places were crumbling at the verges. The aged Morris bumped resolutely towards the McLeish stronghold. The village was only a mile away when the Distillery peeped over the horizon. In London David had made much rueful capital out of his family owning – in a time of whisky drought – a Distillery that had been closed down. The buildings that housed the distilling plant and the warehouses where the hogsheads of spirit were kept in bond, all covered with camouflage paint in one of the General's wartime aberrations, lay empty and disused. The Chinese-shaped cupola that crowned the ventilation shaft was perched at an angle to emphasise that it had ceased to function.

The Distillery, small though it was, had produced a steady income, and there were many reasons to regret its closure. But distilling was an early war casualty: allocations of barley for malting were severely restricted, and the General, as a private owner independent of the big combines, complained that he lacked the clout to get a fair ration. The hands who were of age went off to the war, and the disgruntled owner gave up the struggle. Most of the Distillery's produce had gone south for blending, but a small quantity of 'Old Portree' was bottled each year. The General had prudently ensured that there was enough of the noble spirit in his cellar to last for another Thirty Years' War. The Distillery, David thought as he rattled past the silent frontage, would be sold if he could find a purchaser.

The Chieftain's flag, drooping at half-mast and just visible

14

from the road, reminded him that The Keep was a house of mourning. The lodge at the entrance had been left derelict, its windows blocked with rotting planks. The gardener who lived there had been called up and not replaced. One of the patterned iron gates lay on the ground and a stone pillar had been knocked on its side. David had been at home when the damage was done by a recklessly driven lorry during a Home Guard Exercise. The General left it unrepaired, observing that most gates would be toppled over by Army transport before the war was over.

The famous banks of rhododendrons that lined the drive, untrimmed though they were, offered a defiant mass of colour. The yellows and lilacs of the Alpines nearest the edges were past their best, but the Tibetan pinks and the apricot yellows of the tall Chinese were still in full bloom. Then came clusters of blue hybrids and – the most beautiful of all – the towering mass of the cinnabar-red Himalayans.

David felt warmed by the vivid hues as he pushed open the heavy, studded door and let himself into the Great Hall. A fire blazed in the huge open grate, but there was no one to be seen. His footsteps had a hollow sound. He began to feel that this was a place that had been abandoned. The Keep seemed empty. A humiliating memory came flooding back. His father had taken him, on his first visit to Edinburgh as a boy, to the Royal Scottish Museum. As was the General's punctual habit, they had arrived as soon as the doors opened and made an inquisitive tour of the exhibits, pressing buttons to start the model steam engines into motion, and gazing with astonishment at the prehistoric skeletons. Suddenly David had become aware that they were alone in the vaulted hall. He had felt the monsters descending on him with no one to protect him and his father, and had run screaming into the street. He blushed at the recollection.

His mother and brother were in the sitting room.

'David,' she embraced him tearfully, 'now you're both here. I'm so glad.' She stood in the centre, linking them with her arms. The brothers grinned at each other in awkward greeting.

'Where's, where's father?' he asked tentatively, not being able to think of anything more appropriate.

'He's in the Billiard Room. James Porteous said he had stated in his Will that he was to lie there so that the clansmen could come and pay their respects. Oh, David, they've been coming all day. That's why the fire's lit. There have been McLeishes from Vaternish, and Trotternish, and Bracadale. Even from Portnalong. They've gone now, and left a stillness behind them.' David felt a surge of sympathy for his mother. She had noticed it too. 'They'll be coming from the mainland as well for the funeral.'

David wondered if he was the only one who saw something grotesque in the corpse of the Laird stretched out on the green baize, symmetrically surrounded by the pockets where he had so often sunk the red.

The McLeishes' historic affection for the Jacobite cause had not extended to adopting the Roman Catholic religion. Nor, like many would-be aristocrats, had they joined the Episcopal Church – a moderately revanchist sect distinguished from the national Church of Scotland on grounds more social than doctrinal. Every Sunday at the parish church the General and his family had occupied the Laird's Box, so built that while they could see the minister they remained invisible to the rest of the congregation. On a sunny June day the remains of The McLeish were borne to the simple stone building.

The minister, accompanied by the elders of the parish in kilts or sober serge suits, waited at the church door to receive the coffin. He had been respectfully anxious to comply with past custom and hold a succession of funeral services – in The Keep, at the church, outside when the coffin was laid on the bier to be carried by hand the mile and a half to the burial ground, and finally at the graveside. David had offended the Reverend parson by refusing to allow this Christian harrowing of the mourners. He insisted on no more than a single ceremony at the church (the windows could be opened so that those for whom there was no room within the building could still take part),

16

and the obsequies at the grave.

As he and his brother escorted their mother up the wooden steps to the family seats in the Box, David felt himself an impostor. Respect had to be paid, but he was not a believer, and he had little time for what he regarded as ancient, outworn superstitions. The Psalms sung unaccompanied, the tribal call for aid 'O God, our help in ages past', the celebration of 'How bright these glorious spirits shine', failed to move him. He glanced at his mother, white and tight-lipped behind her veil, and at Charlie who was unashamedly weeping. The General's Commission had been terminated. There were no more obligations to be met. David could not share the grief which he felt was as much for the passing of a way of life as for the person of his late faher.

It was an impressive cortège that wound its way to the Laird's last resting place. Led by the Macleods' hereditary piper playing the saddest of pipe tunes 'Lochaber no more' to recall that the McLeishes had originally come from the shores of Loch Linnhe, the coffin was carried by Estate workers and men from the village. The Guard of Honour from the Camerons flanked it with arms reversed. Behind came David and Charlie, taking it in turn to support the head of the bier. Relations, cousins and other clansmen followed, then the tribute from the Highlands and Islands.

First, the Lord Lieutenant of Inverness-shire, Sir Donald Cameron of Lochiel, Chief of Clan Cameron, tall and upright despite his age, with an eye like Jove to threaten and command, strode forward; the plump, red-whiskered Lord Macdonald of the Isles, whose lands marched with the McLeish territory; Lord Lovat from the Fraser country round Beauly, his martial appearance identifying him as the Commando leader; The MacNab, son-in-law of Flora Macleod of Macleod; The Mackintosh from Moy; Grants, MacPhersons, and representatives from other clans. They marched in their kilts, well worn, possibly shabby to the onlooker, tweed jackets, and plaids over their shoulders. There had not been such an assembly since before the war.

17

The procession slowed as it climbed the path to the place of burial, a square plateau on a small hill between The Keep and the shining river that the late Laird had so greatly loved. The ceremony was brief. The harsh staccato of the Guard of Honour's volley was followed by the lament on the pipes, the pibroch 'McLeish's farewell to Ben More'. A chill wind blew across the open grave and fluttered the eagle's feathers on the Chieftains' bonnets. Despite himself, David shivered. As the column re-formed, marching in quick time to the sound of 'Prince Charles's Return,' he wished he could relate the whole business to a more credible scheme of things, something less like the last stand by the natives in an Indian Reserve. These impious thoughts would, he knew, find no credence, far less acceptance, among those who were now to be offered refreshments in the hall of The Keep.

'I'd like a word with you and Charlie, in private.' James Portous stood at David's elbow.

'Yes, of course. Let's go to the Library. It will be some time before our guests start to leave.'

'Nothing very much, you know, but you've got a lot of kinsmen who will be staying to hear the Will read,' Porteous closed the door behind them, 'so I thought I'd tell you both in advance, as the persons principally affected.' He hesitated for a second. 'Can we sit down? We'll be more comfortable.' They drew up chairs. David had once described Porteous as the arch-stickler, the High Priest of propriety, but today he was not concerned with stickling. He was not his usual brisk, confident self.

'This is very difficult for me, as a friend of the family, if I can call myself that.' David nodded. 'But I'm also your father's solicitor, and what I'm saying now is in that capacity.' He looked over the top of his rimless glasses. 'Your father's Will was drawn up nearly six years ago, on 10th September, 1939, to be precise, just after the outbreak of war. It is a rich man's Will. In particular, it was made before the Distillery stopped operating. Now, the Will itself. First, your mother is well provided for. Apart from some specific gifts, she is to receive in effect the life-rent from the Estate, and freedom to reside at The Keep. I imagine that's what you expected.' Porteous licked his lips nervously. David and Charlie could see he had not reached the matters that were worrying him. 'Then there are what might be called the minor bequests to your cousins and people who are, or have been connected with the Estate. They're all generous, as the Laird would be, perhaps too generous in present circumstances, but they'll be attended to.'

'What about Mrs Macleod?' asked Charlie.

'She's given an annuity and board and lodging in The Keep for as long as she wishes. Now, if I can come to you, David. You're the Laird, the Fifteenth of McLeish, and nothing in the Will affects that, nothing at all.'

'Come to the point, man.' David spoke with unusual asperity.

'I think I had better read the relevant clause. It is as follows:

'To my elder son David, remembering sundry acts of discourtesy I have received from him since he reached what might be termed man's estate, and recalling his undisguised contempt for the habit of life which his ancestors have followed for centuries, I leave and bequeath the contents of the Library in The Keep, being the only thing in which he has shown any interest, provided that the said contents shall not be removed from therein.'

'You realise,' Porteous stopped reading, 'that testamentary provisions written years previously often sound unfriendly and callous when the time comes to enact them.'

'I understand,' said David coldly. 'Please continue.'

'That, I am afraid, is the only reference to bequests to you by name. To you, Charlie,' Porteous hurried on in his confusion, 'is left the whole of the heritable and moveable property in the Estate, subject to two provisos, namely that you should subscribe to the aforesaid bequests in favour of your mother, and that at some suitable time which is left to your conscience and discretion, you should relinquish your Army Commssion and take up residence in The Keep. You are, for all practicable purposes, the new owner of the McLeish Estate.'

'Good Lord! Just like that? It seems so unfair.' Charlie looked from Porteous to David and back again.

'To complete the picture, I should add that in the event of you, Charlie, dying without issue, the Estate passes to David's children, should there be any at the time of your decease, whom failing, to your cousins in Lochaber. There are also some consequential provisions regarding pre-emption. You cannot, for example, sell, dispose of, or alienate any heritable property without your brother's consent, or, if he should predecease you, the consent of his heirs and successors, if any.'

'You can presumably confirm,' David's voice showed no sign of emotion, 'that this Will, which in practice disinherits me, is competent under Scots law?'

'You may remember that your grandfather went to great lengths to break the entail, so that the provisions are perfectly valid. With your permission, I'll leave you together.' Porteous bowed slightly as he gathered up his papers and withdrew.

'David, we'll come to some agreement. Father's mind must have been deranged. That old fool Porteous should never have let him do it. We'll divide it up.' Charlie joined his brother at the window. David shook his head.

'There they are. The great deer forest of Ben More. The mighty Borve river. The defunct Distillery. The Keep itself. God, I hate the lot.' He turned with a thin smile. 'I underestimated the old man. I never guessed he was so wise to me. He's had the last laugh. No, Charlie. I know what you're going to say. I don't hold you responsible, not in any way. But I won't come here again.'

Part One

Chapter I

'What do you know about whisky, Q?' Claude Albizzi, Chairman and Senior Director of Albizzi Brothers, Merchant Bankers, drew fanciful lines on the blotter with his gold pencil.

'Not before lunch, and not with ice,' Quentin Lawrence, the most recently joined member of the Board, answered lightheartedly. He had no idea what lay behind his Chairman's query: he was more interested in Claude's doodling. The sketches he penned in moments of apparent concentration were prized in the office, both for their weird technique and for the possibility that they would throw some light on his inner thoughts.

'I don't mean as a consumer. As an investment prospect.'

'That's not a commodity I've studied in my brief career with Albizzi. I'd have thought it was a pretty safe buy. But surely United Whisky Producers have got it all sewn up, or rather bottled up.'

'They're much the biggest operators, with all their brand names. They call them individual blends, but it's really brand loyalty they're after. There are still some independent distillers who, for a variety of reasons, don't sell to U.W.P. We've been approached by one of them. He wants finance to expand. He also wants help to present the Independents' case to the Board of Trade. Something to do with export licences. Name of McLeish.'

'Isn't David McLeish the Vice Chairman of U.W.P.?'

'He is. U.W.P. winkled him out of the Civil Service after the war, and he's had a rather spectacular career with them.'

'I knew him slightly when I was up at Cambridge. He was older than me. Already a Don doing research. Very brainy, but cold. Known as the desiccated Scot. He was no sporran-swinger. He was the most non-Scottish Scot I've come across. Not wildly popular.'

'That's the elder brother of our man.'

'Then why doesn't he go to U.W.P.?'

'In a word, because it would lead to fratricide. It appears that their father left everything to the younger brother, and all D. McLeish inherited was Scotch Mist. That was about twenty years ago. Now the two of them are more on shooting than speaking terms.'

'The younger one insinuated himself into Papa's affections?'

'That's not clear. But to add a little spice – this is all at second hand – they were both after the same girl, and she spurned desiccated David in favour of young Charles. Since when, no formal contact.'

'What a splendidly operatic story. Deprived of spouse as well as patrimony, he ponders McLeish's Revenge. A libretto for Puccini?'

'More like Hurdy Verdi. A bit of *La Forza del Destino* working its way through the second generation. Would you go and take a look at it? They'll put you up at The Keep. That's the name of the fortress where McLeish peers over the battlements.'

Quentin thought that the morning's doodled sketch would be unusually interesting.

As the train pulled out of Achnasheen, Quentin reflected that it had been partly kindness that had prompted Claude to despatch him to the Highlands. On the face of it, the experience would be useful even if no business was done. It would also be entertaining. Fishing had been promised and, as advised, he had spent a pleasant hour at Hardy's in Pall Mall choosing a salmon rod and reel, and a modest library of flies. So far his angling had been confined to casting a leisurely fly over trout in the chalk streams.

Quentin was also grateful to Claude Albizzi for recruiting him to the firm, but with hindsight the move, if not the actual destination, had been inevitable. Returning to Cambridge after his National Service in the Intelligence Corps, a research and then a full Fellowship in his old college seemed a natural sequence. His father, who encouraged him in his chosen course, envying anyone who could avoid the atrophy of commuting to his accountant's practice in Holborn, had died mercifully soon after cancer was diagnosed. His mother retired to a small house in Jersey and, though Quentin visited her regularly, his father's death left him more lonely than he had foreseen.

It was some time before the academic life began to pall. Unfriends said Cambridge was a cul-de-sac, and he was becoming increasingly frustrated, when a rapid succession of events made him decide to look elsewhere. The first came, improbably, when the father of one of his undergraduates invited him to Newmarket to see his horse running in the Two Thousand Guineas. His host radiated energy. A prosperous Norfolk farmer, he illumined a wide range of topics – from the diastasic content of his barley crop, pheasant rearing, and the iniquities of bureaucracy, to a recent Benjamin Britten concert – with his racy comments. He was a round man. Grasp your problems and squeeze something out of them. That was where the real satisfaction lay. First the blade and then the ear. Organise it right through. Master the machinery and the Ministry and enjoy it all the way.

Quentin asked why he had called his horse, the beaten second favourite, Vronsky. The answer stuck in his mind. Most men would like to have been the Russian Count, to have enjoyed his liaison with Anna Karenina and then been free of her. Vronsky had learned through experience to govern his instincts and would be better disciplined for the future. Quentin took the point. Immersed in the Neo-Platonists, he had only a theoretical solution to offer.

His own amatory episodes had been unsatisfactory. Two harmless early seductions, before he feared he might acquire a reputation for being too intimate with those who came to his tutorials. Then a lengthy affair with a Don's wife. The clandestine excitement gave way to boredom as she became too insistent. Perhaps her aged flesh didn't appeal any more, she berated him. It was not her ripe body, which he still found attractive, that had begun to repel him. It was her mediocre mind, obsessed with the intrigues of Donnish politics.

The watershed came when he realised that his lectures on Castiglione's Renaissance monograph *Il Corteggiano* were not reaching his audience. He had put forward the ideal of the diplomat who was also an accomplished swordsman, musician, poet and lover, as an antidote to the current enthusiasm for sociology as a career. Castiglione's courtier would not only get on in the world; he also valued wit and grace. But Quentin's undergraduates were palpably bored. They dismissed the Italian code of conduct as an outmoded affectation. It was time for a change.

By a happy coincidence Claude had come to address a one-day seminar on finance for industry, and Quentin had sat beside him in Hall. Seeing that his companion was disillusioned with the cloisters, Claude, whose antennae were always keen, asked if he had ever thought of merchant banking. Quentin at first demurred, saying that he was neither an accountant nor an economist: he was scarcely numerate, and he did not think he would qualify for employment behind the counter, far less in the higher ranks. In reply he was given a stimulating description of the scope of the merchant banker's activities and the qualities required. Claude was looking for people who had common sense, who were personable, and who could write. To spare his blushes, Claude went on while the port circulated in the Common Room, knowing that Quentin would score ten on at least the last of these. He had read some of his articles and reviews. Albizzi were presently undermanned. One partner had gone to Schroder Wagg, and another had retired prematurely. The bobby-dazzlers who were being groomed for the future were not yet ready. Quentin was exhorted to think about it and visit Claude in the city if he were interested.

He had not taken long to make up his mind. Luncheon in the Board Room, a friendly discussion afterwards, and Quentin accepted what he considered to be very fair terms.

'I'm glad you've decided to join us,' Claude said. 'I should add that I've consulted my colleagues, and they're of the same view. We don't go quite as far as Warburgs, who take only Classical scholars, but it will be a pleasure to have a distinguished academic on the strength.'

'One of my reasons – not the only one – was your historic name. A firm that antedates the Medici must keep its place in the sun.'

The train was nearing Lochalsh. Quentin took his suitcase and rod down from the rack. His instructions were that he would be met at the ferry. He walked the short distance to the top of the landing ramp, expanding his lungs in the tangy air. Cars were being driven off the newly arrived ferry boat. A girl wearing green cords and a dark blue polo-neck sweater came up to him.

'Mr Lawrence? Cousin Charlie asked me to meet you. My name's Fiona McDhuie.'

'Very good of you to take the trouble. What a marvellous day! After the fumes of London, and a night on the sleeper . . .'

'Look out!' She jumped to pull him aside as a flood of refuse swept past, covering the quay like a giant's vomit. The tailboard of a lorry turning out of the Kyle Hotel had fallen, allowing buckets of swill to tumble down the ramp. Flights of seagulls appeared from nowhere, screaming in their greed as they fought for scraps of food. The air was suddenly polluted with the stench of carrion, fish heads, and offal.

'I spoke too soon. I hope that's not an omen.'

'Not the best of welcomes.' She shook her head. 'You can't fault the scenery,' her gesture extended to the hills in the distance, 'but the by-products of tourism – ugh!'

They picked their way carefully through the sludge to go on board. As the mainland retreated, Quentin saw a dungaree-clad figure descending from the Hotel with a hose. Lustration had started.

'I wish it was always as easy as that,' she said, 'To wash away the remains of visitors, I mean. Sorry. I'm a bit anti-tourist today. The last lot were ghastly.'

It took only fifteen minutes to cross the narrows. The metal landing-plates crunched against the concrete edge and they were ashore.

'Over there.' She pointed to a small estate van. 'I hope you won't find it too uncomfortable. I was determined to see this morning's departing guests off the Island, so I drove them here, and it seemed a pity to use another car as well. The Keep's only a couple of miles from us.'

She said that she and her brother Lachlan had been left Mc-Dhuie House when their parents were killed in a car accident. The only way they could retain possession was to run it as a hotel. They employed a manager throughout the year, and both helped during their vacations from St Andrews University.

'It's a losing battle, really. Cousin Charlie gives us fishing on the Borve at very generous rates. We make a bit on that in the season. For the rest, it's the Public Bar takings from the locals, bless them. Fortunately the nearest licence is sixteen miles away.'

Roadworks held them up intermittently. Fiona looked at the bulldozers without enthusiasm.

'I'm not keen.' she commented. 'Of course we want two lanes, but it encourages the dreaded caravaneers, and they're the bane of the Island. There should be a special cattle-grid at Kyle which caravans can't cross.' After they passed Broadford on the road to Sligachan she described the technique for negotiating the single-track stretches. 'If you see someone coming, you accelerate once you've reached the next passing-place, so that the enemy when you meet him has a shorter distance to reverse. Then you look innocent. It requires great integrity,' she added solemnly, 'and a smile as you sail past. Do you mind if we stop for a moment at Portree?'

Down the cobbles to the harbour, darting aboard a fishing

boat, she emerged with basket of lobster.

'Pity you're not dining with us tonight. But you'll be all right at The Keep. Mrs Macleod will see to that.'

'Mrs Macleod?'

'She's the housekeeper. I sometimes feel that she's been there since the Rebellion. She keeps them up to scratch.'

'What about Major McLeish's wife?'

'Kirsty? Oh, she looks after everyone else on the Estate. Lachlan calls her the Great White Mother, but that's unkind. You'll like her.'

Quentin was anxious to hear more about the McLeish family, but he thought that further questioning would arouse suspicion. Instead, he enquired politely what Fiona was reading at St Andrews.

'I'm doing Economics. One more year to go. Then I think I'll do a Ph.D. on the effect of Scotch Mist on the ecology of the Islands. You know the kind of thing – the prehistoric forests become peat; cattle get steadily smaller, although no one seems to notice that old prints of Highland beasts on the drove roads show a much bigger animal; wars depopulate the villages: and what are we left with? A one-night stand for bus tours from Sutton Coldfield. McDhuie House doesn't take coaches yet, Mr Lawrence, but the end is in sight.'

He studied the slim figure beside him more closely. Auburn hair cut short, deep brown eyes, high cheekbones, a wide mouth and a ready smile. Too purposeful to fit the gamine cliché, she looked younger than she must be. She sounded cynical, but it was clear from the furious way she urged the van along the narrow road that she would go straight at any obstacle in her way. And it was all done with an easy nonchalance he had not met before.

'There's the Distillery. That's what you've come about, isn't it?'

'It looks very prosperous.' The white walls and bright red paintwork glistened in the sunlight. A line of whitewashed stones marked the visitors' car park, and an impressive notice, gilt on black, proclaimed the presence of the Ben

More Distillery. Everything visible within the curtilage had a sleek, well-attended air.

'Cousin Charlie had it all cleaned up. He runs it like a military cantonment. They've got an enormous clock inside, and they're always ringing bells to mark changes in shifts, or something like that. But you'll learn all about it. Here we are at the famous Keep.'

She turned past a trim lodge, along a drive etched by neatly ordered shrubs and rhododendrons, and finally up a semi-circular approach to halt before the entrance.

'Let me do that.' Quentin took his luggage which she had been lifting from the back of the van. 'You've been very kind.'

'A pleasure, Mr Lawrence. We'll meet again while you're here.'

'I hope so.'

'We'll just go in.' She had already rung the bell. Quentin was not prepared for the immenseness of the Hall. It was of staggering depth. The narrow oblong windows were high in the walls. Rounded gold stalactites hung from the green and red pattern of the ceiling. Paintings, pennants, and armorial bearings lined the walls. Antlered heads glared glassily between the suits of armour to give the illusion that a herd of deer had sought protection indoors. The floor was of dark, polished wood. But there was time for only a fleeting glance.

'Mrs Macleod, this is Mr Lawrence.'

'He's expected.' Mrs Macleod was aged; her skin was parchment-coloured, and her hair was white, but her chin was firm and her back held aggressively straight. She carried a bunch of keys, and Quentin felt that he was about to be locked in a cell.

'Will you take tea in the Library, Sir? Major McLeish is on the river, and Mrs McLeish is at the village. They didn't think you'd be here so soon.' He followed her obediently. Tea it was certainly going to be.

He was torn between the tray brought in by the maid – a very male tea of toast and anchovy paste, scones and jam, and some treacly gingerbread – and the books that lined the shelves. It was an impressive room with its heavy curtains and rows of morocco, calf, and Russian leather bindings. Above the book-cases were portraits of bloodthirsty Highlanders. Quentin deduced the bewhiskered warriors to be McLeishes, although it was difficult to detect any family resemblance beneath the foliage. There was something uniform about their attitudes and the texture of the paintings that argued great tenacity of purpose over centuries, or a single retrospective commission. More probably the latter.

Clutching his toast, Quentin inspected the nearest shelves. This was the Sporting section – *From the Hoogly to the Googly*, the Badminton series, *Adventures in Grouseland*, Scrope's *Art of deer-stalking*, Waddington on salmon, and the volumes of Colonel Peter Hawker. Then works on Estate management, forestry, and farming. William Forsyth, J. C. Loudon, Philip Miller and Arthur Young were all represented. An Indian enclave, no doubt reflecting an Imperial tour of duty by an earlier McLeish, displayed the Memoirs of General Havelock, Kaye's Afghan War, *The Court and Camp of Runjet Singh*, and *Sindh and the Indian Races*. One wall was given over to bound copies of the *Quarterly Review*, the *Gentleman's Magazine*, *Blackwood's* and *Country Life*, and to fiction. Scottish authors – Smollett, John Galt, Stevenson, Scott – stood rank by rank alongside other predictable writers, Dickens, Jane Austen, the Brontës, Henry James. Quentin was surprised to see Scott-Moncrieff's translation of Proust (that must have been a sport, or a female McLeish), and the works of Ford Madox Ford.

It was not a scholar's library. There was no sign of a bibliophile in the family, but individual interests had left their mark and the catholicity of taste showed how self-sufficient it was intended to be. For the remote Highland Laird, books had long been the only recreation throughout the stark winter months. Quentin remembered William Beckford acquiring Gibbon's library against the distressing possibility of not having enough to read in Lausanne.

Beside the fireplace hung a contemporary painting of Lord President Forbes of Culloden who had tempered with judicial mercy the painful task of sentencing loyal adherents after the

31

'45. 'Patron of the just, the dread of villains, and the good man's trust.' As he read the rhyming rubric, Quentin thought it very likely that he would be asked to drink to the King across the Water.

'Mr Lawrence, I'm so terribly sorry. No one here to greet you.' Quentin saw a tall, broad-shouldered, heavily built man in tweed knickerbockers and a Norfolk jacket with fishing flies stuck in the lapels. Balding, with his remaining black hair brushed across his forehead, a round rubicund face and moustache just under control, he smiled his welcome. 'I'd meant to be back sooner, but I was lucky this afternoon. Two beautiful grilse, seven and eight pounds. I lost all comprehension of time till I landed the second one. You've been warned about fishing, I hope? Good. The river's in pretty fair shape. A bit low, but there's a fresh run of fish and you should have some sport tomorrow. My wife's about one of her good works, but you'll see her at dinner. Good heavens, I'm being a dreadful host.' He lifted a decanter from the tantalus on the side-table. 'This is poor Highland hospitality. You'll have a dram to mark your arrival?' Quentin nodded. 'You see that hellish device?' McLeish pointed to the tantalus. 'It's meant to have the crossbar locked to keep the servants from tippling. My father bought it and ceremoniously threw away the key. Since God has been kind enough to give us the Distillery, he said, let us enjoy it. I believe it's the Papacy in the original quotation.'

'Leo X. I prefer your version.'

'Slainthè. But no more talk of whisky just now.'

'I was admiring your library. Have you a record of when the various acquisitions and additions took place? It would be very interesting historically.' Quentin had more than history in mind. He was intrigued to learn what interest this hairy Highlander had in his extensive collection. He looked very much the archetypal Laird, but there was an old saying that the habit does not make the monk.

'History, Mr Lawrence, is something we need here like a hole in the head. We can't get away from it, but my job is to make things work.' He struck his right fist into his left palm. Then, it

32

seemed to Quentin, his host realised he had spoken more forcibly than the conversation required. He might have given something away, and that, as he fixed his slightly beady eyes on his guest, was not his intention. 'Look at the McLeishes round this room,' he continued more equably. 'My grandfather had all the portraits done by Sir Alexander Grant. He was the fashionable painter of the time, but the objective was to make sure that my father, I and my sons, and their sons after them don't forget that in the beginning there was a McLeish. Admirable in its way, but they', he pointed upwards with his glass, 'didn't have to worry about central-heating bills, or capital gains tax, or the other exquisite torments that face us.'

'All country houses are having a bad time.'

'You shouldn't confuse us with the country house in England. There the feudal barons didn't run to a single, permanent home. They lived in one of their castles for a time, ate all the local produce, and then moved on like locusts. Or they clustered round the Court in London. Later, when the jovial boys were reduced to a single residence, it was an exotic new building, with a formal garden *all 'Italiana*, and parks dotted with lakes, obelisks and suchlike. The English country house was always imposed on the countryside. It did not emerge from it.'

'That's a highly individual, but most interesting view. You say the Highland experience is different?'

'Entirely. The Keep is not divided from the landscape, not even by a ha-ha. It is where the family lives. This, I say it with all due modesty, is the centre for all those who have their being round it. Originally they were members of the same clan or family. Many of them still are, and the village consists largely of people working on the Estate, or in the Distillery. Rewarding, but it does create the most hellish obligations. But that's enough Highland theology.' He got up.

'Anyhow, I'm very envious of your library. It's so beautifully arranged.'

'You're too kind.'

'This is a subject on which I could claim a little expertise. Who did the indexing?'

'Sorting out the books was the work of the great brain my brother – or rather of the student he sent to compile the catalogue. The Library, unlike the rest of The Keep, belongs to him. He wanted to be sure we didn't start flogging it at Sotheby's.'

Chapter II

Towelling himself in the spacious, Victorian-tiled bathroom, Quentin felt that residence at The Keep was full of hazards. He had nearly drowned. His eyes and nose were still tingling.

After a second glass of whisky and a walk through the gardens – more onions than oleanders nowadays, his host explained – he had been pleased to find his clothes laid out. Someone, he suspected the minatory Mrs Macleod, had decided that a blazer and dark checked trousers would be suitable. He remembered McLeish saying that they would not dress and that there would be no other guests. His bath had been run, and he looked with approval on the steaming water, tinted with the colour of peat, softer to the touch than in the South. Inserting his toes in the taps, as his custom was, he lay back luxuriating in the warmth only to sink at once beneath the bubbly surface. The bath was much longer than he had realised and the sloping end was out of reach. Floris soap, peaty bathwater, and the lingering taste of malt whisky were not an agreeable mixture, and inhaling the hot liquid made his nostrils smart. He cursed the earlier McLeish whose gigantic frame had required a vat of such mammoth proportions.

The bath, on drier reflection, was an heirloom, but one that remained in use. In London it would have been prized as a collector's piece, or as a facility for bisexual orgies. The distinction might be seen as a symbol of the difference between life among the McLeishes and in the Square Mile. Put another way, could there be more of a contrast than between cool Claude, backed by his graphs and abstruse calculations, and the florid Charlie striving to cope with anachronisms that obstinately survived? It was Quentin's job to find a common denominator. In theory, he had to decide whether the Distillery figures afforded a viable basis for a loan, but that could almost be done by correspondence. Claude also wanted his views on the man, whether he was someone to be underwritten for the sizeable amount involved. This was the kind of problem Quentin had looked forward to when joining Albizzi, but he had not foreseen that it would take such an acutely personal form. Castiglione had prescribed a certain prudence and wise discrimination in applying courtiership. This was going to be needed.

Charlie found him looking at the contents of a display cabinet in the Great Hall.

'These', he said, 'are our sacred Jacobite relics. The blue bonnet was the one the Prince threw in the air when he raised his standard at Glenfinnan. The silver hairbrushes and the looking-glass were left behind in Skye when he was hunted off the Island. There are appropriate stories about the presence of McLeishes at each stage. You'll observe that the trinkets are all below glass.' He tapped the front of the case. 'That's where they should be. Preserved, conserved, locked away. But we still have visitors whose piety would not disgrace the most devout pilgrim when he reaches Mecca.'

'I expected more enthusiasm for the House of Stuart.'

'Between ourselves, the Stuarts were born losers. They couldn't survive. But they have their uses. We romanticise them. They stand for a régime committed to care for the Highlands, and that's more than can be said for our present legislators. And', he added with sudden bitterness, 'we have other forces to contend with in South Britain.'

Charlie, who had changed into a green velvet smoking-jacket with a tartan collar, led his guest into the sitting room. Introduced to his hostess, Quentin saw at once why she had been pursued by both the brothers. Tall, with enormous blue eyes and a fresh complexion, her dark hair at shoulder length was held by a dark velvet band. She wore a white silk blouse and lace jabot with a large Cairngorm stone set in a silver brooch, and a long royal blue skirt. She had a warm presence, and as she held out her hand Quentin thought it would be ungallant to think of the term well-preserved. It occurred to him only because he knew she must be at least forty. She was very beautiful.

'I hope you're comfortable in your room?'

'I am indeed. I've already', he added with a laugh, 'done a couple of lengths of the bath.'

'You sank in the Tub? Many of our guests do that. Charlie, you should have warned him. We call it Tammas's Tub. He was a large McLeish last century. He had the bath installed when he made a lot of extravagant additions. Apart from the Tub, they've all been demolished.'

'Were they all as eccentric?'

'Very nearly. He built the most awful excrescences. In the middle was the Billiard Room. Underneath, some obsolete offices – the pastry larder, the lamp room and the brush store – and on the top floor there was even a sitting room for the visiting valets. Hideous from the outside, all studded with corbelled towers. A great day when it all went. We put in central-heating at the same time. Hurrah!'

'An expensive operation, my dear.' Charlie did not share her pleasure. 'We had to sell our Allan Ramsay portraits to pay for it. They weren't as good as the Red Macleods that hang at Dunvegan, but I was sorry to see them go. My brother was very difficult about the sale. I should explain, Quentin, that I can't sell any heritable property unless he agrees. Strictly speaking that didn't cover the paintings, but as they were valuable I thought it courteous to consult him. It was a mistake.'

'Charlie, you're exaggerating. He was trying to be funny.'

'I think not. He replied through his solicitors, saying that the disposal of ancestral baubles was a belated sign of grace before The Keep finally sank into the peat-bog.'

'Give Quentin another Martini, and do stop grouching. There are plenty of snags to running this ancient monument, and fraternal sarcasm doesn't help.'

'I imagine the Hall itself is a problem?' Quentin was trying to be helpful.

'Who wants something like Alexandra Palace in the middle of their house?' Kirsty made a face. 'The Prince Consort once came here and the McLeish of the time taught him curling, throwing heavy granite stones up and down the Hall. It took months to remove the scars from the floor. Think of polishing that acreage by hand. Now it's treated with silicone and only needs the electric polisher once a week. There's no labour-saving device I haven't tried.'

'Kirsty's very good about it, but you can't get staff with any sense of dedication nowadays. We'll never replace Mrs Macleod.'

'Dedication to slavery, you mean, darling. Of course they won't work all day in stone-flagged kitchens – though at least we've renewed them – or sleep in bedrooms like closets in the attic, placed as far away as possible in case they try to creep away for a nap in the afternoon. We're lucky to have anyone left, and I think Mrs Macleod is sometimes too hard on them. For myself I don't mind. Keeping the house and the Estate going is what keeps me on the move. Whatever I die from, it won't be torpor.'

During dinner Quentin was enchanted with Kirsty, from the disarming way she disclaimed responsibility for the game pâté and the salmon steak, saying that Mrs Macleod approved the cook's proposals once a week, to her gentle attempts to rouse her husband from the gloom that seemed to have settled on him. He suspected her task must be a hard one when they were alone.

He liked too her graceful comment that their Visitors' Book nowadays recorded a diminishing number of old friends, so that she enjoyed having Quentin on his first – with a clear infe-rence that it should not be his last – visit. She had the rare gift of making her guest feel immediately at ease. But Charlie was not to be kept off his subject for long.

'I read in *The Times* that some bimbo in the Lords had the nerve to rejoice that the day of privilege had gone. The big landowners were doomed. No turning back the clock. All the usual guff expected from Life Peers. Archie Strathgarve tried to argue that there were still family Estates that were not dead, only moribund, thanks to the greedy disposition of the Chancellor. But he got thoroughly snubbed.'

'That's Archie all right.' Kirsty rose from the table. 'Some people are born to be snubbed. He's one. Anyhow, it's only jousting – unless there's money involved. Now, Charlie, I expect you want to take Quentin off to your office. Don't keep him up too late. He's had a long journey today. I've got some telephoning to do.'

'My wife', Charlie made light of her concern, 'is deep in a domestic drama. The daughter of our head ghillie Angus Cameron has been left in a delicate condition. The youth who went shooting out of season has fled to Invergarry to work on the Hydro-Electric scheme. But he didn't reckon with Kirsty. She's arranging to have him returned.'

'When I was certain that Morag wanted him back,' she added, 'not just her father, it seemed the best thing to do. We don't want to lose young people from the village if we can help it. But I sometimes feel that we don't run the Estate. It's the Estate that runs us and dictates what we do.' Her smile indicated that she was not averse to accepting her lot.

Quentin was surprised at the up-to-date equipment in the office – dictaphone, electric typewriter, the latest duplicator, fitted filing cabinets, and a large-scale relief model of the McLeish lands and territories.

'I expect you thought we still used quill pens and a sand-horn?' Charlie gave an awkward laugh. 'We've got all the gadgets and gimmicks. Efficiency, that's it.' His voice rose. 'I should say, first, that I'm very grateful to you for coming here. We'll go over the figures in due course, but there will be other things you want to see. Don't comment, but I know you will have to assess my credit-worthiness, and that of the Estate. Quite right, too. So let's have a look at it.' He moved over to the model. 'There's The Keep in the middle. To the west lie the Macleods with their castle at Dunvegan. Between us there's a

39

tongue of land belonging to the McDhuies which runs up to Loch Dhuie. But they're mainly to the south and they haven't much left. On the east, the Macdonalds, towards the Storrs and Portree. On paper I'm a large landowner. Thousands of acres. But you can see that apart from the strips on either side of the Borve River it's all peat and rocks. Not even the satraps at the Scottish Office have cobbled up a P.N.P.'

'Meaning?'

'Peat National Product. But I've turned what I can to profitable use. There's the Home Farm. About 8,000 acres. Run by McLeish Farms who lease the land from the Estate. Ownership of the company has been transferred to my two sons, so there should be no difficulties about tax on succession. My wife and I draw Directors' fees, and there is a saving there since they count as earned income. Our cars are charged to the farm, and all our staff appear as farmworkers. Long may the normally searching eye of the Revenue overlook this beneficial arrangement.'

'Not much arable, I see. What do you rear?'

'Cattle. When I took over it was all scrub. Breeding cattle on the hill was becoming the vogue, and there were three pioneers in the Highlands – Lovat at Beaufort Castle, Duncan Stewart of Millhills, and Joe Hobbs at Inverlochy, near Fort William. Joe's conditions were nearest to mine in climate and soil, so I went to see him. He took me in his yacht to Ireland and introduced me to the man who sold him his Kerry blacks. I tried the same thing, and it's worked well. We do a bit of cross-breeding now, and we've got 400 head wintering on the hill. Calfing percentage is high, and I sell the calves once a year. Special train from Kyle. T.V. and all the publicity I can muster. With sales, the calf subsidy, and the reclamation grants, we show a modest net profit.'

'Very enterprising, but what do you feed them on in the winter? Hay will be difficult in your wet climate.'

'You're so right. It's pathetic to see crofters trying to dry out their pitiful crop. If it ever does dry there's no protein left. Silage is the answer. I make 2,000 tons a year. On Joe Hobbs's advice I've tried everything from Russian Comfrey to lupins. The locals thought I'd finally gone mad when they saw a field of bright red lupins. Challenging, but it's damned hard work. We reclaim a hundred acres a year, ploughing and seeding, but unless we keep at it, the bracken and rushes come back.'

'The old proverb about the pitchfork and nature still winning.'

'Yes, but I'm going to win.' He glared defiantly at Quentin before continuing.

'The east side of Ben More, the more sheltered side, is laid out to trees. This qualifies for a grant from the Forestry Commission under their dedication scheme. Forestry, at any rate for the present, is treated very favourably by the Revenue. Useful when the time comes to pay my death duties', he added grimly. 'Even there we could claim to be as efficient as anyone. The Commission have made a lot of progress with planting on peat. I've fitted our mechanical plough with a new track which we've invented. It covers terrain that used to be inaccessible. Beat that. Ho-ho!'

Quentin found it impossible not to be infected by his enthusiasm, although the tenseness of his delivery made it less attractive than it would otherwise have been.

'Then there's the river. Apart from a rod I keep for my guests and myself, the boats are leased to McLeish Sports Ltd. Kirsty's the Chairman. She sublets to the McDhuies for a nominal rent, so that they can advertise fishing from the Hotel, and for the rest we get upwards of £100 a week for each rod. The income from McLeish Sports goes straight to the British Virgin Islands and so doesn't attract income tax.' There was no disguising Charlie's gratification at this fiscal ploy.

'Lastly, all our shares in these companies, and the Distillery, are now owned by a Lichtensteiner anstalt, an open-ended trust which has special tax advantages of the kind you will understand. I had a dreadful job persuading our lawyer James Porteous – he was Kirsty's uncle – to agree to that one. It was the last thing he did before he went off to present his final balance sheet beyond the skies. It may have hastened his decease, I'm afraid, but it's been very lucrative.' Charlie laughed immoderately at the recollection.

'Strategically, that's all very sound. I'm beginning to doubt that you need any advice from Albizzi.'

'That will become clear later. Meanwhile I'm going to give you some more Old Portree.' He refilled Quentin's glass. 'You can taste the peat in it. All the Skye whisky is like that. Talisker which is the best known, has a slightly milder flavour, not so pronounced as the ones from Mull. Laphroaig, from Islay, is the heaviest of all, is the drink to separate the men from the boys. I've always been proud we're mentioned in the whisky ballad.

'Glenmorangie, Glen Livet,
Hear the Holy Highland chant:
Portree, Laphroaig and Talisker,
Glenfiddich and Glen Grant.'

Any questions on my presentation so far?' Charlie seemed to be reaching a euphoric stage. Quentin was aware that the exposition he had heard, casual though it appeared, had been carefully thought out to show that the Estate was both well managed and profitable. Whisky had been introduced as a diversion.

'I'm most impressed.' This was intelligent husbandry, outwith his experience. All the assets had been harnessed, and Quentin was far from clear how he was going to make his assessment. 'Apart from the Distillery accounts which we'll look at in detail later, I would like to see a summary of the revenue from other sources. One thing that does interest me is how it looks, say, over the last five years. When you've got time. Don't put yourself out.'

'That can be done. I wouldn't pretend it's easy to maintain profitability. Sometimes it's a dreadful strain.'

A purple vein stood out alarmingly in his forehead. 'I remember one morning, soon after I had resigned from the Army and come back to The Keep, watching the mist rising from the peat hags and thinking, why bother? Why not stop shaving and reach for the bottle? There was plenty of Old Portree in the cellar. Then I thought what an ass I'd be. Beaten without firing a shot. So I buckled to, and no carping critic in London is going to stop me.' He emptied his glass. 'Time to turn in, if you're ready. The form tomorrow is that you should fish the river all day. It's falling already, and unless we have more rain there won't be another chance so good. Then we'll have a talk in the evening and on Wednesday we'll do the Distillery. I have to be in Portree for a District Council meeting, but I'll take you down to the river before I go, and Angus will look after you.'

'Good morning, Jessie, Mr Lawrence is going to catch his first salmon.' Mrs Macleod had come to the door as Charlie and Quentin were loading the gear in the Land Rover.

'I hope you'll be lucky, Sir, and that they won't have to name a pool after you, like the Doctor.' The smile was polite, but there was a glint in her eye.

'Jessie, you're being mischievous.' As he started the engine, Charlie explained that the Doctor was a physician who had been drowned fishing one of the deep pools. He had been found with his line wrapped tightly round his wrist. A salmon had taken his fly, pulled him off balance, and he couldn't recover himself or free his hand. He had been dragged towards the bottom end of the pool and had gone under. The pool had been called the Doctor's ever since. 'Jessie was being helpful in her sly way. Two morals to that sad story. Don't wade in the Borve by yourself, and keep some loose line but don't let it coil round your hand.'

Although it was a summer day, a fire burned in the fishing hut.

'We stack enough peat outside before the season starts, and we keep it smouldering from then on. It's very convenient when you come cold or wet off the river. Makes our tenants think they're getting their money's worth.' He chuckled with feigned avarice. 'The only trouble is that Angus has to come down on Sunday to back up the fire.'

'It's just as well, Sir.' The ghillie's voice had a soft West Highland cadence. 'It gives me a chance to see if there are persons who are fishing on the Sabbath. Can I have a look at your flybox, Sir?' He had assembled Quentin's rod, noting its suppleness and strength without comment, and run the line through the rings. After examining the contents of the box with indifference, reluctant interest, and finally with resignation, he closed it with a decisive snap. 'We'll try a Captain Bob' He took one from the sleeve of his jacket. 'That will let them know we're here. You were saying you haven't done any salmon fishing before. It's much the same as trout, but it's a heavier rod. Don't take it back beyond the perpendicular, and let the rod do the work. We're going to try greased line.'

'That means you work the fly a different way?'

'Indeed it does. The last ten or twelve feet of your line will float, and you'll see the fish coming to the fly. Don't hurry him. Say "God bless Prince Charlie" before you tighten. Otherwise you'll take it out of his mouth and he won't come back. Now, in here, Sir. Cast well across at forty-five degrees from the shore. Let the stream swing you right round. They lie quite close to the bank.'

Throughout the morning Quentin applied himself zealously to carrying out Angus's precepts, but he met with no success. The flies were changed. The bushy Captain Bob gave way to the brightly coloured Jock Scott and in turn to the yellow of the Garry Dog. There seemed to be no shortage of fish to mock him. A silver salmon would leap from the water, landing again with a nonchalant, almost contemptuous splash. These, Angus emphasised, were not 'taking' fish. It was the quick, barely perceptible head and tail rise which signified one that might be interested.

'I can't say they're very aggressive this morning.' Angus's admission struck Quentin as a notable understatement. 'But sometimes they change their minds. We'll do this pool again with a Shrimp fly, and then it'll be time for lunch. I think you're moving the fly too fast. Mrs McLeish does the same. A very keen fisher, and lucky too, but she goes too hard at it. You'll feel it in your back by evening, Sir.'

'I suppose Major McLeish casts a long line?'

'He does that, but he always has something on his mind. It's seldom he relaxes to watch the water – like yesterday when he had two beautiful fish.'

'It's a heavy responsibility running a big Estate.'

'And he makes a good job of it.' They were sitting on the bank while Angus tied on the Shrimp. 'But there's one thing. You may have heard the saying that at every Highland meeting there's something that isn't mentioned. It hangs above the table like a cloud that's been blown across the Minch from the island of Harris. Everyone knows about it, but no one says anything. It's like that with Major McLeish. Only it's worse. It's not something. It's someone.'

'I don't quite follow.' Quentin was being deliberately obtuse.

'I'll tell you what, Sir.' With the fly secured he bit off the spare length of the nylon cast. 'It's his brother. Major McLeish owns the Estate, but he's not the Laird, and he won't let anyone call him that. It was a malicious Will their father made. His elder brother who lives in London is the Fifteenth Laird, and they say he looks down on the Major.'

'How can he despise his brother? It sounds like sour grapes.'

'It could be that. But it makes the Major determined, I would have to say unnaturally determined, to make a success of it. He'll be doing himself an injury before long. There you are. Give the Shrimp a float and see if it'll attract them.' He made it clear that he had said enough.

The Shrimp was only marginally more successful than its predecessors.

'I felt a touch,' Quentin exclaimed.

'You did that. There was a fish at your fly, but he didn't really want it. We'll take that as a hopeful sign for the afternoon.' Quentin felt another tug and concentrated more fiercely than ever on casting.

'There's Madam with the lunch.' Angus pointed with his gaff to the Land Rover coming down the track. As she stopped, Kirsty made interrogatory signs through the window. Quentin shook his head ruefully.

'Never mind. A blank morning's always entered up on the

45

credit side. You'll do better this afternoon. Isn't that right, Angus?'

'Yes, Ma'am, sometimes.'

Quentin admired her elegant appearance – fawn tweed culottes, dark-green knitted stockings and a pullover to match. While the ghillie helped her to unload the luncheon basket, he could not help overhearing the brief conversation that passed between them.

'You've to meet the Portree bus this evening,' she said. 'Iain will be on it. I've heard from Invergarry.'

'Ma'am, I'm very grateful.' Angus's voice was thick.

'My husband will see him in the morning.' She placed a comforting hand on his shoulder. 'We'll put him on forestry, and there'll be a cottage vacant before too long.'

With a stimulating dram of Old Portree, some nourishing soup, Mrs Macleod's cold game pie, and most of all Kirsty's company, Quentin began to forget his morning's frustration.

'I feel I'm here on false pretences,' he said. 'I've done nothing to earn a day like this.'

'Not a question of earning.' She gazed thoughtfully at the tips of her brogues. 'I can guess what you talked about last night.'

'Second sight?'

'Not even intuition. It would be penal taxation, the perils of dry rot, and the impossibility of getting staff. Right?'

'In part. We did talk of other things. I am fascinated by the expert way Charlie has organised all his affairs. He has got tax avoidance down to a very fine art.'

'Tell me this. Will the whisky exercise result in a conflict with David?'

'It might. But not necessarily.'

'If it does, I want you to discourage him from going ahead. I don't want anything that will lead to a fight. It's not worth it.'

'I see. There would be too much of an emotional strain?'

'There would. I've got a husband I love, a household I can just manage,' she looked him straight in the eye, 'and two adorable sons who're away at school – I'm sorry you haven't met them – and I don't want everything upset by Charlie and David

46

getting at each other's throats. I don't give a damn about the Distillery.'

'It has some financial advantages, or could have.'

'To my mind they're not important. Charlie's thinking of what he can pass on, but the boys will look after themselves. There's a lot to be said for them making their own way. And despite the Celtic gloom we all suffer from, we're not down to our last bottle of Old Portree yet. Have some more.'

'I'm a professional adviser, possibly an agent if the whisky negotiations develop, but I'll remember what you say, and I'm honoured by your confidence.'

'Now,' brushing off the crumbs, she stood up, 'Angus is going to see that you catch a fish. Aren't you, Angus?'

'That depends, Ma'am.' The ghillie had eaten his lunch at a respectful distance. 'Not on Mr Lawrence, nor on me, but on the fish. And who knows what they're thinking?' He made it sound like an incantation. 'We'll try a smaller fly. We had size 8 this morning. We'll go down to size 10. If that doesn't work it would need to be a trout fly and a prayer at St Columba's.'

'Don't let him discourage you, Quentin. What beat are you going to do?'

'We did the Upper Borve stretch this morning, Ma'am. We'll try the Laird's and then Prince's. And that'll be it.' There was an ominously final sound to his reply.

The Laird's pool, wide with a dark, almost oily surface, proved unproductive. Angus opined that the water was too low for the places where the fish lay if they were within range. They hurried down to Prince's, and Angus instructed him, with more precision than before, to cast on the edge of the rough water. The stream would bring the fly round behind a large submerged stone. That was where they would be.

'I've got him!' Quentin started as his line tightened. He had seen a movement in the water and waited obediently for the prescribed interval.

'You have, Sir. Come nearer the bank before he runs. The shingle is a bit treacherous where you're standing.' Quentin stumbled to shallow water. Then his quarry ran. Right across the pool to the far side. He felt the friction of the line burning his fingers. He reeled in as the fish came back towards him, keeping a steady strain. The salmon leapt in the air. Quentin lowered his rod point to bow to him lest the nylon should snap. For a quarter of an hour he played his adversary. The singing reel made music in his ear and his excitement grew. The fish began to tire: his sorties were shorter; he was nearly finished. Quentin felt a moment of intense pleasure – the combination of the river rippling past his waders, the salmon, tight on his line, lying down the path made by the sun's reflection, and the clouds rushing over the tree tops – which he would not forget.

'Short line, Sir. Walk slowly backwards. He'll come after you and land himself.' Angus stood beside him with the 'priest', a loaded club, in his hand. 'That's it.' The white belly showed. He was beached, open-mouthed and gasping. Angus despatched him with a merciful blow.

'Congratulations. You played him right bonny.' He put his spring-loaded scale in the fish's gill. 'Twelve pounds. Fresh run. Still with the sea-lice on him. I thought for a minute you might lose him when he started sulking.'

'I didn't like that vibration when he tugged in jerks.' Quentin was babbling with relief and achievement.

'But you finished him off well. Life's never the same after you've caught your first salmon. Yes, I'll have a dram, seeing it's an occasion.'

Quentin proffered the bottle which Kirsty had left. They drank in satisfied silence.

'Tell me, is Mr David a fisher?'

'He never comes to The Keep now. The last time was when his mother died. He arrived the morning of the funeral and left immediately afterwards.' Angus seemed about to say more, then thought better of it. 'I don't think we'll be seeing him here, Sir.'

48

Chapter III

'I don't agree that he's as calculating as you make out, darling. I found him rather sensitive.' Kirsty was brushing her hair in front of the bedroom mirror.

'Despite all that polish, he's pretty shrewd.' Charlie contemplated his favourite view of Ben More. 'He's a Cambridge Don turned merchant banker. Must be very versatile to change horses like that. He doesn't seem terribly interested in the details, but he's sizing us up. I can feel it.'

'We haven't had a nicer guest for a long time.'

'Callous at the end of the day, I should imagine. He reminds me a little of David. Icily polite. Always watching. That may be significant when we go to the Board of Trade. I expect D. McLeish will be active on the other side, so Mr Lawrence may be very useful.'

'Don't, Charlie.'

After soaking, uneventfully, in the Tub and dressing at leisure, Quentin made a telephone call.

'Claude.'

'Hullo. Have you mastered the mysteries of the usquebaugh, if that's how they pronounce it?'

'I don't know about the pronunciation, but it tastes all right. I caught a salmon. Distillery inspection tomorrow.'

'Splendid. How do we stand on personalities?'

'Doom-laden. They've got a bit polarised in the last few

49

years. Now they're increasingly uncordial. There are signs of efficiency in plenty, but it's too emotional.'

'I've got something on emotions for you. The desiccated one, the fellow you knew at Cambridge. Do you follow?'

'Yes. U.W.P.'

'He's suddenly burgeoning with emotion, maybe with something else.'

'I don't believe it.'

'Oh yes. The sap is rising. Let me put you in the picture. We act for Sammy Sacher, the cosmetic king from New York. You haven't been in on that, but you will be when you get back. He's taking over Aphrodite Products – Love in a Lipstick and all that mild erotica. The funny part is that U.W.P. own Aphrodite. It was their first and most unsuccessful diversification. It's not their line of country. They are anxious to sell and your man is in charge of the negotiations on their side.'

'But what is the personal involvement?'

'One of Aphro's assets is a contract with a promising film star, or rather starlet might be more accurate,' Claude could never refrain from that kind of assessment, 'to model for them. Your hero, who has been taking a keener interest in Aphro in view of the proposed sale, has gone overboard for her.'

'January and May? He's too long in the tooth, surely?'

'Wait. Sacher has a majority share in her latest film, and there are rumours that she may be his protegée, to put it delicately.'

'Perhaps that will distract Big Brother enough to keep him from opposing our little scheme here, if it comes off.'

'I doubt it, but further research on the kinship won't be wasted. Enjoy your *villegiatura*. Take your time – within reason, of course.'

The evening sparkled. There were three other guests: Fiona, her brother Lachlan, and the venerable, white-haired General Havelock Carnoustie. Kirsty was the accomplished hostess that Quentin by now expected, and her husband was in a much more cheerful mood. But it was Fiona who shone. She wore a

clinging dress of apricot jersey, and it was impossible to be unaware of her lithe, attractive figure. Quentin felt it would be
easy to be bewitched.

Carnoustie, who was an annual visitor to McDhuie House
for the fishing, described how he had caught a salmon on the
Lower Borve beat.

'I had to do some strenuous Spey casting to entice him out of
his lair under the trees. Then what did the rascal do? He came
at me quicker than I could shorten my line. I do believe he was
hostile. So I gave him the command "About turn" and he made
off downstream.'

'Don't believe a word, Quentin.' Fiona laughed. 'General
Havvy always shouts at the fish. If you were near him you'd
think you were at Chelsea Barracks.'

'Anyhow, he was obedient. Took his punishment like a good
sporting fish. I understand this is your first visit to these parts,
Mr Lawrence. If you take my advice, you won't be bam-
boozled by these devious Highlanders. They make everything
more difficult than it is, so that their miserable success will be
enhanced thereby. If they can't catch a really big fish, they'd
rather not catch one at all. No use your willowing about to distract me, Fiona. Flies on the water. Keep your nerve. That's all
there is to it.'

'What about the blank days last week?', Fiona asked inno-
cently.

'Kirsty,' he replied, 'aren't you going to give your old friend
another sharpener? And keep your water-sprite under control.'

Scouring the barrel of his memory. Quentin recalled that
Carnoustie had been known as a blade in his earlier career.
There was a story about firing a Verey Pistol from the Mess
while the Duke of Gloucester was dining. The War Office had
not liked it. Now mellowed in retirement, with a Rubens touch
in his complexion and humorous lines round his mouth, he was
still capable of dominating those immediately round him, and
very likely to do so.

Fiona recounted Carnoustie's first appearance at McDhuie
House. She had persuaded Lachlan to advertise the hotel in the

51

Sunday Times. By some statistical mischance their first batch of guests had all, except for the General, been obvious abstainers. Lachlan had said they could make out their bills in advance because they wouldn't spend anything in the bar. As they sat in the drawing room that served as a visitors' lounge, primly sipping their coffee, the atmosphere had resembled a geriatric ward ready for inspection. When she had confessed her disappointment to Carnoustie he had at once offered to stir them up.

'An abstainer is an affront to the deity,' he intervened. 'A little persuasion and they soon reached the rank of postulant. I started them on sherry, then *vin rosé*, then claret, and by the time they left they were lapping up Old Portree, I expect they're all in an inebriates' home by now.'

'Apart from making teetotallers into alcoholics,' Quentin suggested, 'it must be fun running a hotel here. You have one of the idyllic retreats everyone covets.'

'I didn't think you'd be so naïve.' Fiona smiled slowly. It was not easy to meet her gaze. 'We do well for a few weeks in the summer. Even then, unless they want to fish, or stalk, or climb – and we're too far from the Cuillins for those who want to risk their limbs – there isn't all that much for them to do. We feed them well, though we couldn't match Kirsty's noble dinner tonight. We wouldn't give them sea trout as well as venison. Lunches are no problem. The shivering guests are issued with sandwiches, made in the winter and kept in the deep freeze, and driven out into the rain. Special rain. Much wetter than anywhere else. If they're reluctant, Lachlan asks them condescendingly if they're game, and that usually clears the lounge. When they come back, soaked and weary, we guarantee hot baths. Then they collapse without resistance. We're full for the Skye Gathering, but after that the bedrooms are empty, and by the end of September there's not a single visitor left. Then we live on the Public Bar till the next Easter.'

'Any accountant would say we were mad,' Lachlan continued. 'Ours usually does. In a well-run hotel you should have an annual occupancy of about 65 per cent. We hardly reach that during the summer months, far less over the whole year. Your bar takings should not run to more than 40 per cent of your total income. I would hate to tell you what percentage ours reaches. We'll keep going for a bit longer, but if we're faced with any major repairs we're sunk.'

'You amaze me.' Quentin liked Lachlan's common-sense attitude. It confirmed his frank, open countenace. He had already explained he was in his fourth year as a medical student, and intended to be a surgeon. A more pragmatic person than his sister. 'I should have thought the Highland mystique was more marketable. For example, he turned to Charlie, 'have you considered opening The Keep to the public?'

'Often, and always rejected it. This is a home, not a museum. We've nothing much to show – only the trinkets in the glass case – and I don't fancy giving lectures on family feuds. Flora Macleod does this business very well at Dunvegan, but they're a numerous clan who've been thoroughly indoctrinated to make pilgrimages to their tribal shrine. She's got far more to offer, both inside and outside the Castle. If we tried to compete we'd only queer her pitch, and I wouldn't want to do that. Good luck to her!'

'Charlie's absolutely right,' Lachlan agreed. 'It would be a a mistake for him to go for tourist traffic. We're too small at McDhuie House and we need two things. We want something for people to do in the evenings, or when the heather is too damp for a bit of swizzer-swozzer. That means some civilised amenties at Portree, which is not so very far away. We also need more accommodation, preferably chalets. They would cater for the more discerning who don't want to be stapled into coach tours, but can't afford hotel prices. We'd still get them in the bar. It's not a good proposition for risk capital, but I've some hopes of the new Highland Development Board. They have all the powers, if they use them. I'm sorry Charlie was not asked to serve. Instead, they've appointed some town planner as Chairman.'

'Charlie can count himself lucky,' was Carnoustie's comment. 'Anyone read Lampedusa's novel, *The Leopard*?'

'I have,' said Quentin, 'but the relevance escapes me.'

'You remember the passage at the end when the fellow from the Cavour Government comes to the Sicilian Prince and says they want to post him as the first head of the new Sicilian Development Board? The prince replies that the Cavour boys haven't done their homework. The Sicilians are convinced that they are perfect, and therefore incapable of improvement or development. Moreover, from the moment they are born they are obsessed with the death-wish, and all they want is to be left on their tod till the time comes. So the Prince applies for permission to fall out. If you substitute Highland for Sicilian, you get the whole thing in a nutshell. You're well out of it, Charlie.'

'Dear General Havvy. So depressing, but such style.' Fiona leant across and kissed him on the cheek.

'If the Board's a non-starter, what's the answer?' Quentin asked.

'Whisky from the Ben More Distillery.' Charlie's remark was greeted with shouts of derision.

'There isn't one,' Kirsty spoke up. 'We're in a cleft stick. We keep up a standard which many people would envy. They contrast it with the lot of the crofter who can't live on the produce of his croft and has to leave the Island. Incidentally, there are not many crofters who work as hard as Charlie. But, not to be too smug about it, suppose you have a tremendously keen social conscience. Suppose you divide up the whole Estate among those who live in the Parish of Borve. What would happen?' Kirsty was the one who took their badinage to heart.

'It would be derelict in a decade,' said Charlie.

'I don't know.' Kirsty shrugged her shoulders. 'I think it might. But to my mind, if the community is to stay, we've got to stay. The Keep's the focal point. That, Quentin, is why Charlie has to run the Estate as professionally as you've seen.'

'I think Havvy', Fiona put her arm round his shoulder, 'should make amends for being so discouraging. I propose to appoint him G.O.C., Anti-Jacobite Forces. We know the Edinburgh Festival is subsidised by the Military Tattoo in the Castle. As soon as the Festival's over, the troops should be

54

marched to Skye to re-enact the death throes of the '45. A great lifelike historical pageant. The T.V. audience would love it. General Carnoustie, Sir, you've got a new Command.'

'Not me, my dear. I'm on the War Graves Commission, and that's my last job. Besides, if you were to be realistic, you'd have to leave half Prince Charles's troops asleep in Inverness, as they were when they should have been on the battlefield. If there's to be any pretence to accuracy, it would come out that only two Chiefs were actually killed at Culloden. The rest were agile or absent. Very embarrassing, I dare say.'

'I didn't know you were a Jacobite scholar.' Charlie was still surprisingly relaxed. There had been no reference to his brother throughout the evening. 'But you'd better be careful about voicing these heretical opinions. Where did you learn this?'

'Believe it or not, many years ago we did an exercise on the '45 campaign at the Staff College. Fergie Callander was in my syndicate, and I was so astonished at his views that I haven't forgotten them.'

'I'm not going to give up.' Fiona made a face at him. 'If there's no future in tourism, or the Highland Depopulation Board, or a Jacobite frolic, there's only one thing left. The Venetian solution. Now. Quentin, what is it?' He was as much aware of the challenge in her eyes as in her voice. 'A distinguished Italian scholar should know,' she taunted him.

'Venice? Silent rows the silent gondolier. Her palaces are crumbling to the shore. No. *Mi dispiace*. I'm baffled.'

'You disappoint me. We announce with a great fanfare that, like Venice, Skye is sinking. All the cloud-capp'd palaces, Dunvegan, The Keep, Armadale, the Cuillins and the crofts will soon disappear into the peat-bog, and there will be nothing left but a fine crop of bog myrtle. Your last chance to see the lone shieling on the misty island. Walk up, ladies and gentlemen. Make your bookings now. One more opportunity to drink Old Portree and stay at McDhuie House.'

'That is where I'm taking her,' Lachlan interrupted, 'before she gets herself lost in a further flight of fancy, and we all have to go out and look for her.'

But Fiona had one more *pas-de-bas* before the entertainment was over.

'Will I see you again before you go?' she asked Quentin.

'I don't know. Tomorrow I spend at the Distillery, and I should go South on Friday.'

'Charlie, you mustn't let him leave without getting a stag. If you will lend me Angus, I'll provide the pony.' She turned back to Quentin. 'Will you come with me? Do stay another day. You'll still be back in London before the weekend's over.'

Kirsty assured him this was a serious invitation. Lachlan and Charlie had other things to do, Lachlan at Raigmore Hospital in Inverness, and Charlie as Honorary Sheriff Substitute at Portree, but they both emphasised that Fiona had a keener eye on the hill than they had.

Quentin went to bed with a warm glow, not entirely due to Old Portree, permeating his limbs. He had been tempted to say that the stalking invitation was like the bizarre custom of Cesare Conzaga's cardinal who put his visitors at a disadvantage by making them strip and try to beat him at jumping. And the evening's symposium had reminded him of Castiglione's entourage touching lightly on subjects whose seriousness belied their facetious description. He must put Castiglione from his mind. He had an immediate job to do. But Fiona was as lovely as the elegant Emilia Pia who had enchanted the Court circle at Urbino.

Chapter IV

'Have a seat, Iain. I hope you're glad to be back.' Charlie spoke hurriedly to cover his embarrassment. Iain Shearer sat on the edge of the chair, his hands on his knees. There was no response in his cold, unblinking, blue eyes.

'I'm not so sure. I liked it fine at Invergarry. The pay was good, and you could get to Inverness or Fort William at week-ends. I'd have stayed, but the gaffer made it clear he'd been told to lay me off. Then the Manager, he said I wouldn't get any work on the Hydro scheme. That's no way to treat a man.'

'I'm sorry you feel like that. But you have responsibilities here, you know.'

'I'm not very certain about that, either. I'm not the only one that's been there. Like bees round the honey pot, they were, after the ceilidh. And I wasn't the first, either.'

'Morag will make a good wife, Iain. Angus will have told you we'll let you have Ben View, though it's normally a stalker's cottage. We'll do it up for you.'

'That's obliging, very obliging. It's a handy place for the village, and near the Distillery, too.' He stared Charlie full in the face.

'Good. That's settled, then. Full time on forestry. Piece-work on fencing till the end of the year, or as long as the weather holds. Then we'll give you the average till the Spring.'

'That's a wheen less than the Hydro paid, but it's fair.'

'And you can do a day on the hill, if you like.'

'I'm not having that. The rate for the job, that's all. I won't be like Old Angus, doffing my cap to city slickers pretending to be sportsmen. Besides, I'm thinking Morag will be left enough on her own while I'm away on the other side of the Ben. That's not a good thing for a young married woman.'

'I won't press you, if you feel like that. I hope you and Morag will be happy, and that you'll enjoy Ben View.' He stood up. Iain sat studying the palms of his hands before he rose.

'Do you smell the malt?' Charlie asked as they dismounted from the Land Rover in front of the Distillery office. 'You can always tell when we're distilling. A good, rich, mature smell.' He sniffed again appreciatively.

'What are these?' Quentin pointed to a cluster of huge sheds which lay behind the main building. Hidden by a fold in the ground, they were, despite their size, invisible from the main road.

'These are the bonded warehouses. That's where the whisky's kept till it matures. We'll go and inspect one presently, when I get hold of the Exciseman. He has to be there when we open the door. That's in case we whip off a barrel duty-free. Meanwhile, note that they don't disfigure the landscape as most warehouses do. This is starting at the wrong end but, as I'll explain later, part of the plan is to double the warehouse capacity. Luckily, we've plenty of room, though there'll have to be some excavation. But they still won't be noticeable, so the planners will not be awkward about giving permission. Normally, they put up a series of diabolical hurdles, but this time there won't be any steeplechase. There are no problems about drainage or landscaping, and they can't argue for long against the prospect of additional employment.'

'I notice there don't seem to be many people about.'

'There aren't a great number. Whisky's a disappointment so far as providing jobs is concerned – though it's good for the employer. In all, we have thirty men here. If my scheme goes through there will be nearly twice as many. That would employ everyone in the village and the immediate surroundings. Too tidy to be true.' Charlie had all the details in his head. It was something he had lived with for a long time.

'This is Norman McKellar, the Distillery Secretary.' Quentin shook hands with a small, dark, sharp-nosed man in a well-pressed tweed suit. 'He's been here ever since we reopened after the war. He's known locally as Old Portree. Is that right, Norman?'

'That's right. Sometimes as Mr Whisky as well.'

'Are you a Skye man, Mr McKellar?' Quentin was making conversation.

'Yes, but I'm the only one of the family that still stays here. I've got a brother who went to London to be an accountant with Margraves, the West End store. We're negotiating to supply them with a special House brand – that's if the expansion comes off. But my brother's a hard man to deal with.'

'Here, Quentin, is a masterly schedule which Norman has prepared. It's more self-explanatory than these statements usually are, but I'll add a few comments. This is a Malt Distillery. What we make is a pure malt.'

'The one that makes manifest the works of creation,' McKellar grinned. 'Not to be confused with the proprietary brands.'

'Exactly.' Charlie continued. 'Section II gives the output figures. Except for a small quantity which is bottled for my own use, and some which we sell to McDhuie House, it goes to Glasgow for blending with grain whiskies. The blenders may want it at any time – provided it's at least three years old. Section III sets out the oncosts, and there's a balance struck over the page in Section IV.'

'At first glance, 'Quentin was still studying the figures, 'it looks a neat, prosperous concern. I can quite see why you want to expand, but from what you said yesterday it's not just a question of raising output?'

'No. The idea is to add a grain still, and work it together with the existing pot still at full capacity. We would put in a bottling plant and market a new blend under our own name. As you can imagine, this would not be well received by our main competitors.'

'Meaning U.W.P.?'

'Principally. They don't like distilleries that are not tied to them – particularly since they embarked on their own expansion on Speyside. Given a chance, they'd probably buy our plant as it stands, and close it down. They almost certainly wouldn't take our product for their own blends. If we're to expand, we've got to do it on our own – and there are two major obstacles.'

'Both created by U.W.P.?'

'In effect, yes. The first is the three-year rule. Thanks to pressure from U.W.P, the Board of Trade will not let anyone sell whisky before it is at least three years old. There is no magic about this, and I would defy you to tell the difference between whiskies at two, three, four, or five years. Many overseas countries, in South America for example, will accept imports of two-year spirit on an analyst's certificate, which is a much more objective test. So you've got the absurd position of an eager, thirsty market abroad which we can't satisfy because of U.W.P.'s restrictive practices. Now we come to the second way in which they hamstring us. The warehouses.'

'This one beats me.'

'If we make more and it has to mature in bond for three years, we will need far more warehousing space. There is the cost of erection, but that can be found. Much more sinister is the high insurance premium which would have to be paid, and the fact that the distillery has to finance a fidelity bond to cover the value of the whisky in store. That is a large sum.'

'This is the value before excise duty is paid on withdrawal?'

'Even so, it is large. These are the figures. Thank you, Norman. Column 7.'

'But this is a reputable venture in trade. Surely the banks will provide some accommodation?'

'Not on reasonable terms. I don't want to impugn their integrity. No doubt they can find good, commercial reasons for their attitude. But the views of U.W.P., who are enormous customers – and often represented on the Boards of the Clearing Banks – are clearly taken into account. That's where you come in.'

'I see. The problem is to find the capital to finance the expansion and cover the three years in bond.'

'That's the picture. To my mind it makes sense only if we can make the Board of Trade reduce the statutory period from three years to two. Then we can sell overseas. That's absolutely essential if we're to start a new brand. We'll never break into the home market on our own. We're not big enough to compete with the household names.'

'So you want us to tackle the Board of Trade and also see what the money market looks like – all with U.W.P. lurking in the background?'

'And you know who the Vice-Chairman of U.W.P. is?'

'I assume you're not counting on any support from your brother. But will he actively oppose you?'

'I'm afraid so. He hates everything to do with the Estate. There is no doubt that he can get U.W.P. to do what he wants. One nod from him and U.W.P. will hamstring us.' Charlie's pathetic expression revealed how strongly he felt about his brother's attitude. 'That's why I called in Albizzi. Let's have a walk round while you think about it.'

Quentin had the whole distilling process demonstrated, from the floors where the fermenting barley was regularly turned by wooden spades to prevent bruising, to the drying over the peat reek in the kiln. Then came the first wash and the final distillation which produced the elixir. He wondered at the onion shape of the vast copper and admired the silent way in which everyone went about their work. The Exciseman joined them in No 1 Warehouse, and Charlie explained that the hogsheads marshalled on either side of the aisles were originally sherry casks. This was supposed to improve the flavour. The wood drew any imperfections from the contents, leaving a dark rim inside the barrel. That in effect was maturing, which ceased when the whisky was bottled.

'One question, perhaps a very foolish one, is why the Distillery is here, in this particular place. Your raw material comes from the mainland. Wouldn't it make more sense to have your plant in say Kincardineshire where the Golden Promise barley

61

you use is grown?'

'The choice of the original site was probably accidental. When private pot stills were banned, the Laird of the time managed to get a licence to keep his own one going. Then it expanded in the absence of any legal competition, and once it had started it was going to stay. Eventually everyone became convinced that the peculiar flavour – and Old Portree has a flavour of its own, as you've seen – depended on the whisky being distilled on this very spot. There are many theories why this should be so. Some say it's the air, or the angle which the hillside presents to the sun. I'm fairly certain it's the water. It has to come out of peat and flow over granite, as it does here.'

'What is surprising, Mr Lawrence,' McKellar added, 'is that when they moved a Distillery on Speyside only a few hundred yards they found the whisky tasted quite different. One thing is certain. It has to be made in Scotland, though the Japs have the impertinence to market a beverage which they call whisky from the misty glen of Yamazaki!'

'Perhaps it's best that it should remain a mystery. You said you hope to start a new blend. What imaginative name will dignify the label?'

'I've always wished I could revive the title "Ferintosh",' Charlie laughed. 'The story is that Lord President Duncan Forbes, whose picture you saw in the Library, was allowed to choose his reward for his labours after the '45, and asked for the produce of the distillery of that name to be exempt from excise duty. A grateful Government so decreed, but before long the Treasury lit on this objectionable anomaly, as they saw it, and the privilege was withdrawn. What was Burns's poem, Norman?'

> 'Thee, Ferintosh! O sadly lost!
> Scotland, lament frae coast to coast!
> New colic-grips, an' barkin hoast
>   May kill us a';
> For loyal Forbes' charter'd boast
>   Is ta'en awa'!

McKellar intoned the rich Doric with evident pleasure. 'But', he added, 'if we can't have that, the Major's minded to call our whisky "Dew of Ben More" which has a good ring about it.'

'All single syllables,' Charlie agreed. 'That seems to be important. Most of the best-selling brands are monosyllabic. Meanwhile, you must have a dram of special Old Portree. This', McKellar poured three glasses, 'is twenty years old. From our first year after the war.' Quentin savoured the smooth quality of this princely drink.

'Makes the basest man bless his enemy.' McKellar's quotation was clearly one he kept for the occasion. With some justification, Quentin thought.

He suggested he might browse over the figures for an hour or two in the afternoon. He needn't detain Charlie, but it would be helpful if he could call on McKellar for any additional information he required. Charlie, realising it was his absence that was wanted, readily agreed.

Quentin found himself warming to McKellar. His enthusiasm for the Distillery was very apparent, and the bird-like way he nodded his head to emphasise his answers gave them added conviction.

'I don't want you to think I'm an accountant, Mr McKellar. I'm not, and I'll have to take most of these papers away for further study. On the face of it, however, your whole project is viable, more than viable. It will be very profitable if we can get the three-year embargo reduced to two. That won't be easy. On the other hand, a more modest expansion would pay, irrespective of the three years, since you wouldn't have such an acute storage demand. Why not do that? There are far fewer risks.'

'That's a sensible question. The answer's got nothing to do with accountancy, or profit and loss. What I'm going to say is in confidence, but I take the view that you should know the whole story. We could go ahead with a smaller scheme, and U.W.P. in the person of Mr David, couldn't stop us. But that wouldn't do for the Major. He's got to face his brother and get the better of him. He knows he may see the whole proposition founder, but it's all or nothing. That', in profile, McKellar's nose was oscillating as sharply as a woodpecker's in an attempt to drive his point home, 'is also an infuriating Highland trait.'

'He wants to carry the fight to the enemy's ground, does he? Courageous, but maybe foolhardy.' Quentin was sorting out the papers he wanted to keep.

'It may well be', McKellar nodded. 'It's a pity he's so obsessed with something that happened a long time ago. He's a good employer. Look at these cottages.' Through the window a neat row of whitewashed buildings could be seen perched at intervals along the side of the burn. 'He keeps them all in good repair, and the rents are minimal. He's just given the nearest one to Angus Cameron's daughter and her husband-to-be.'

'That's Iain who's returned from Invergarry?'

'News travels fast. Major McLeish may regret his generosity. Iain's a ne'er-do-well. He'll get drunk and fall in the burn on his way home. Morag's a flighty one, too. A beauty, and she knows it. She used to work in the office here, but she wouldn't make any attempt to do the books properly – or even turn up if she didn't feel like it. Major McLeish fired her when I told him it just wouldn't do. She made a terrible scene. I heard it through the door. Luckily the Major's not easily diverted once his mind's made up. Now, if you're ready. I've to take you to Mc-Dhuie House, where Mrs McLeish will pick you up.'

It was Lachlan who greeted him.

'Well met. I'm going to zero this Mannlicher for tomorrow. Care to come? It won't take long, and Kirsty's not here yet.'

Zeroing was soon completed and Lachlan declared himself satisfied with the grouping on the target.

'Have a shot or two at the dummy stag's head.' He gave Quentin the rifle. 'It will let you get the feel of it.' Quentin fired several shots, then handed back the Mannlicher, admiring its balance and smooth action.

'Let's hope you get a shot tomorrow,' Lachlan said encouragingly as they went back to the Hotel. 'I'm sorry not to be with you, but Fiona's a lucky stalker. Seldom returns with a clean barrel.'

They found her at the Reception Desk.

'I've passed the test, I hope. Lachlan has declared me competent to bear firearms.'

'There, Lachlan. That wasn't so clever. I knew he'd see through it. Lachlan said you weren't to be let loose till he was satisfied you weren't a public menace. I was willing to take my chance.'

Kirsty arrived to drive him back to The Keep. On the way, she said Fiona had taken a great liking to him. She wasn't always so forthcoming.

'Fiona's my dearest friend. Although she's much younger than me, I feel closer to her than almost anyone. And don't let her fool you with all her dramatics. She can't help it, but despite all her bright remarks she's not really so sure of herself. Why do you laugh?' Quentin shook his head. He was tempted to say that he found the patterns which the inhabitants of Borve wove round each other were more enthralling than the finances of whisky production. He had not seen Fiona as a soubrette. The airy grace which she diffused was a refreshing contrast to the melancholy undertones he detected in Charlie and suspected in Kirsty, and she appeared to invite him to admire her candour. Now Kirsty had suggested that nothing was what it seemed. He had some deep thinking to do.

Chapter V

For the first time, Quentin saw the unrelieved majesty of the Cuillins in the morning sunlight. The higher reaches had been obscured in mist since he arrived on the Island, and he had learned that this was the customary state of things. Now the gods had relented. Save for a single ball of cotton-wool floating lazily over the highest peak, the whole serrated range lay patent to his gaze. The ragged rocks presented a formidable, forbidding appearance. They challenged the traveller to find a way through, past, or over them. But today anything might be possible, and the deer forest lay elsewhere. A final glimpse from his lofty window, and he went down to breakfast.

Fiona, driving the now familiar estate van, was prompt on her hour. Angus was already in the back. Something of her excitement was apparent in the way she forced the van over the muddy tracks down to the river, across the hump-backed bridge, and up to the croft where the pony and its attendant were waiting.

There was no delay in transferring the gear to the panniers on the animal's back, or in setting off in single file, with Angus leading, then Quentin, with Fiona and the pony boy in the rear. Angus identified a distant ridge and said they would lunch there; the deer forest was two further crests beyond. They made their way round the shoulder of Ben More on paths through the forestry plantations, then on increasingly rough ground as they climbed towards their first objective. Angus halted at regular intervals, but Quentin, who had thought himself moderately fit, was soon sweating. Angus advised him to take off his pullover and put it on again when they stopped. The air was colder at the higher altitude, he added, waving with his stick at the skyline.

Fiona found a convenient gully for lunch and motioned Quentin to sit beside her, sheltered from the wind.

'Penny,' she said, as she offered him another salmon sandwich.

'Sorry. I was thinking the worthy General called you a watersprite. But this is your real element. On the hill, I mean.'

'Possibly. I like stalking as much as anything. Is that unnatural, do you think?'

'I had a niece who came back from Kenya and applied for a post as Researcher at the Imperial War Museum. When they asked her why she thought she should have the job she replied she was quite handy with a rifle. They were so surprised they appointed her. So, who knows, it might come in useful. It's perfectly natural, if you live here.'

'But I won't be able to stay. As Lachlan said, only for a year or two at most. A real dilemma, Quentin. I simply can't think of not being here, but if I stay much longer I'll become part of the scenery, like Kirsty.'

'I suppose that does happen to her.'

'Inevitably. She'd be a *mem-sahib* herself if she wasn't such a kind, generous person. She's absolutely tireless, and so loyal to Charlie. It's not just because she's married to him. It's partly to prove to herself that she made the right choice. Charlie's my cousin, and of course we all adore him, but he's not really the world's most attractive man, and he's getting rather paunchy. Whenever Kirsty thinks of this – and she must, though she'd never admit it – she becomes more determined to prove she still loves him, and sometimes she overwhelms him with affection. Sorry. This is all third-year psychology.'

'Sprites are always full of sensibility.'

'You know about the great feud with brother David. She puts him firmly, oh so firmly, out of her mind. From what she's told

67

me, David tried to make the running. Then Charlie returned from abroad and swept her away. This is only a hunch, but I think he won just because he wasn't David. As simple as that. But I wonder if she ever regrets being stuck here instead of being married to a rich man in the south. If she does, even subconsciously, there must be a hidden feeling of guilt.'

'Even so, Charlie does well out of it.' Fiona might be ingenuous. Anyone older would have been more reticent. But he did not query the accuracy of her appreciation.

'But sometimes it's too much for him. I don't think he can cope with all that unquestioning affection. Was it Flaubert who said the real tragedy is to be loved too much? I don't want to labour this, but I suspect he in turn feels ashamed he can't respond to the all-embracing nature of Kirsty's feeling for him. That's what caused the flurry with Morag. You needn't pretend ignorance. I saw you pricking your ears when Iain's name was mentioned at dinner.'

'That accounts for the gift of Ben View.'

'Partly. There's nothing in it so far as Charlie is concerned. No more than an odd day after woodcock, to use one of his favourite phrases.' She imitated Charlie's throaty delivery.

'Does Kirsty know about this lapse, or lapses?'

'She never will. At least I don't think so. If Morag tried anything, the village would crucify her. Iain's the problem, but he knows where his bread's buttered. No more gossip. Angus, are we going to be lucky?'

The ghillie had made a crutch for the telescope with his left hand and the stick which he had driven firmly into the ground between his legs. He sat studying the landscape for some time before he replied.

'The deer are in the forest, Miss Fiona. There's himself on the ridge, and there are five more, not far below him. They've got their heads down, and they won't move unless they're disturbed. One o'clock from Callum's Point. Have a look yourself.'

'That's him!', she exclaimed. 'He's a real beauty. Is the wind all right? We'll have to go down the line of the burn.

68

Here, Quentin.' She pointed to a prominent white rock in the far distance. 'Just beyond the Point. You'll see him.'

Adjusting the lens, he saw the grazing herd. Their skin was lighter, redder than he had expected. They were utterly at peace. They had no idea they were being observed by predatory man. He felt a stirring within him.

The scene before them was desolate. The ridge where they were sheltering descended to a plain, divided by a burn wide enough in its later stages to be called a river. Increasing in breadth, it was fed by a tracery of small tributaries before winding out of sight behind the foothills. The terrain was covered by an irregular pattern of bracken, heather and rushes. Advanced soil erosion revealed deep brown gashes where the peat lay bare. Nearer the river, leonine rocks added another dimension. When a glimpse of sunlight between the fleeting clouds brought a patch of heather into sudden focus, its sensuous purple served to emphasise the bleakness of the surroundings.

Fiona had warned him that although the first part would be straightforward, the ground in the strath was marshy and treacherous. Then they would keep under cover of the burn till they reached the hillocks before the Point and the ridge where the deer were to be found. The order of march had changed. Fiona was now in the lead, with Quentin between her and Angus. The pony boy was left behind. A handkerchief waved from Callum's Point would be the signal to bring the beast to meet them and assume its burden.

At one of their infrequent halts Quentin asked who Callum was.

'He was an early McDhuie. Like many subsequent ones, he was short of working capital. He paid court to a wealthy McDonald heiress, but she would have none of him. One night he crept into Portree with his clansmen and raped her at the point of the dirk, while his pipers played to drown her screams. The McDonalds weren't too pleased. They're supposed to have summoned their clansmen, then chased him to yonder Point, where he was surrounded and cut to pieces. It's folk-lore now. They still tell it at the village school.'

69

'Point steak?'

'Tartare, more likely.'

'They didn't teach that at school.'

The passage along the burn side, crouching where the bank did not provide enough cover, proved increasingly strenuous and he envied Fiona's agility.

'Down,' she hissed, flopping in a clump of reeds. Quentin collapsed obediently to find the stream pouring into the top of his knickerbockers and down his legs. A glance over his shoulder confirmed that Angus had found a drier resting-place. An aged black-faced sheep was gazing down on them, though without any particular interest.

'If he takes fright,' Fiona whispered, 'the deer will get the message, and they'll be off. We'll have to wait till he moves.'

For half an hour they remained in their damp lair till the sheep kicked up his heels and padded away. From now on the advance was slower, by fits and starts, much of it in the prone position easing forward on the elbows. The Point, when they reached it, was much more massive than it had appeared through the telescope.

Angus crawled up and peered cautiously round the bluff. He came back nodding with approval as he unslung the rifle.

'They're just round the corner. Stand up and fire as soon as you're ready. Take him that's nearest you. You'll get but one shot.'

Quentin looked towards Fiona. 'Good luck,' she mouthed at him. He edged round the rock. Then he rose and fired at the brown mass in front of him. As he squeezed the trigger he knew what he had done. He had shot at a petrified tree trunk, in colour and outline like a grazing stag. The deer who had been obscured by the shoulder of the Point were further up the hill. They stood surprised, staring arrogantly at him.

'Reload. Fire again,' Fiona shouted in his ear. But it was too late. They had gone, with their rumps bobbing contemptuously over the skyline.

Quentin sat with his head in his hands.

'What can I say? I feel such an idiot.'

'It's not everyone that gets a stag at the first attempt,' Angus consoled him.

'Don't worry. It was my fault for shouting at you.' Fiona put out a comforting hand. She had taken off her jerkin. Her breasts were clearly outlined against her shirt. Quentin suddenly wanted her. It wasn't only the deer he had been chasing, he realised.

'I suppose that's it for the day. What do you think, Angus?'

'I can see three on the side of Ben Dearg. We'd have to go round the face of the Cauldron. If you're thinking it's worthwhile we'll need to hurry.'

'I'm game.' Quentin would have stalked the length of the Island to atone for his error. They set off with renewed briskness, and although it was a difficult traverse they kept up a better pace than they had earlier in the day. Most of the climb was across the rim of a semicircular, concave feature where the bare face afforded only a treacherous foothold, but they felt they were closing on their quarry. As they gained height they moved with more circumspection and Fiona, who was once more in the lead, kept low as she clambered under cover of the projecting rocks. They found the remains of a sangar – a few stones heaped together by a stalker or a shepherd – and cowered behind it.

'I'll just go forward and have a look at them.' Angus returned shaking his head. 'They're really too small.' He looked at them both. 'But if you want a shot . . .'

'What would you do, yourself?' Fiona asked.

'I'd be taking my hat off to them to say good afternoon.'

Quentin knew the decision that was wanted. He rose; the others followed: for a second they faced the young deer.

'Halloo!', she shouted. A couple of bounds and they disappeared over the ridge.

'Now that we're here, let's go to the top.' Quentin led them to the summit. They were now at the highest point and the panorama encompassed the hills known as Macleod's Tables round to the Old Man of Storr. Loch Snizort and the sea channel of the Minch lay on their left, and to the other side an unrelieved series of crests in echelon. The heather was broken by a pattern of small lochans and one larger narrow loch which gleamed in the sunlight.

'What's that one down there called?'

'That's mine,' she answered. 'The boundary between us and Cousin Charlie goes slap through the middle of it, but he always calls it Fiona's Loch. I used to come here and fish for trout, but it's a long march for a small basket.'

'And what's that shed doing on the bank?' He pointed to a derelict hut at the end of a track running to the water's edge.

'Prospectors. Not very successful, I'm afraid. There's some stuff called diatomite in the bed of the loch. There was an attempt to extract it, but thanks to the wettest summer of all time, lack of capital, and transport difficulties – though you can get quite near it from the Portree road – it didn't work. In short, a typical Highland exercise.'

'No more Celtic gloom. It's too good a day.' He lay on his back, relaxing.

'Tuppence, this time.' Fiona knelt beside him.

'"Queen and huntress, chaste and fair." – Ben Jonson must have had you in mind.'

'Quentin, how gallant. I've enjoyed today. I really have. Even if you didn't gralloch your first beast. Come on, Angus. Home.'

They started on the long descent, halting only once.

'I hope I haven't given you the wrong impression.' She turned to him. 'About Kirsty and Charlie, I mean. Why they're not in such complete accord as they should be. It's not simply the ghost of David. There's another aspect. All Charlie's interests, the things he plans for the Estate in that dreadfully determined way, come from his own ideas. He's thought of them, and carried them out by himself. He's imposed his will on The Keep and its surroundings. Let's be frank, he's imposed his wishes on Kirsty as well. She's not an unwilling subject. But the whole thing's one-sided. Charlie's only one stage removed from prehistoric man who shuts his mate in a cave – or a Keep. That wouldn't do for me.'

Not much was said on the return journey. Steam from their clothes and the acrid fumes from Angus's pipe misted the windows of the estate van. Quentin, his face smarting from exposure, could hardly keep awake. His head kept banging against the door. He woke with a start when they pulled up at The Keep. Fiona said she had a thought, a second thought. If Quentin did not have too much to talk about with Charlie, why did he not come and dine at McDhuie House? It would be good for him, she added tartly, to see how the other half lived. She would speak to Kirsty.

This she had done. An hour or so later, bathed, changed, with that agreeable sense of well-being that comes from physical exertion, Quentin found Kirsty ready with a dram of Old Portree as consolation for the elusive stag. Fiona had asked them all to dinner, but Charlie had been delayed at the Sheriff Court, and she would stay behind to wait for him. Quentin suspected that this had been an invitation meant to be declined, but Kirsty's opaque comment was that he was almost a resident now.

The evening stayed in his memory. Fiona, radiant in a long skirt of McDhuie tartan and an almond-coloured top, was keen to show him the full enormity, as she put it, of the Victorian mansion. It was built to the order of a McDhuie who had been a Nabob in India. He had sent home instructions that a suitable property was to be prepared before he returned, racked with malaria and, in Lachlan's terms, with his liver curried. Fiona was not sure whether it was the architect, who had taken more trouble with the kennels than with the kitchen quarters, or the Burra Sahib who had covered the walls with ornate oak panelling and cluttered the rooms with heavy brass fittings, who had been most to blame for leaving a thoroughly unmanageable ménage. But, she pointed out with pride, she and her brother had tried to transform it. They had cleared out the oriental bric-a-brac. The study, with the woodwork stripped to show off the original scarlet silk wallpaper, now served as a hospitable bar. That and the Public Lounge at the back – the only extension

73

they could afford – was where the hotel revenue mainly came from.

Quentin said that it was clear that she had not only studied political economy at St Andrews. She also knew all about domestic economics. Maybe, she replied, but they had sunk all their capital. They could do no more. They would have to wait till the roof fell in, or the obsolete wiring sent the place up in flames. She did not want to leave. She would be heartbroken if they had to go, but, for different reasons, she felt as much a prisoner as Kirsty did. Then there was Lachlan. When he passed his medical exams he would have to practise elsewhere, but she felt she had a duty to keep a base for him. So, she added, it was not as simple as it seemed. Quentin was touched to see how fragile she was, despite her bright-eyed, beguiling manner.

Over dinner, a wholly satisfying meal of smoked haddock mousse, tender pink lamb and syllabub, they talked of other things – hotel guests who cleaned their shoes on the curtains, or who, incredibly, preferred sliced bread imported from Glasgow to her own home-baked loaves. Not till they reached the sitting room, their one private place as Fiona described it, did he detect another strain in her make-up, in the person who was casting a spell on him. He noticed the watercolours that lined the walls. They had all been done by her father. Painting had been his obsessive interest. Of course he was an amateur. He had been at the Scottish Bar, but had not greatly enjoyed it. When the war came he had joined the Camerons as the most unsoldierly of officers, had been wounded at Alamein, come home, married her mother, reopened the House, and spent his time sketching, fishing, and walking the moors. There had been enough money then.

How had he got on with the inhabitants of The Keep, Quentin asked? They had been friendly, although her father had never been intimate with his cousins. They talked fishing, but her father was too quiet for Charlie who could not understand his apparent lack of purpose, or his disenchantment with the clan totems. She had heard of an occasion when Charlie – there had been other guests present – had asked who was the greatest piper of all time. This was to give him an excuse to dilate on his hero the first MacCrimmon, an Italian called Petrus who had come from Cremona, hence MacCrimmon. Her father said he understood that Nero and the Duke of Windsor had both been experts. This was true, but it was not thought to be a proper response. Her father had been a kindly, compassionate man. She remembered the first time he taught her to sniggle a trout. No one disliked him, and she loved him very much.

Her mother was a Lowlander from the Borders. She had not found translation to Borve congenial, but she was completely wrapped up in her husband. Whatever he needed, she was at hand to provide. If he had one of his attacks of asthma, she was ready with the Friar's Balsam. When she was not attending to her wifely duties she was intent on her knitting and sewing. She really believed that Satan found work for idle hands, and the tapestry that covered the chairs was the result of long, patient hours with the needle. But Fiona never heard her give an opinion, except to endorse her father's views. She was invariably submissive. Poor dear, she did not know a great deal about motor cars. She could only distinguish between a Bentley and a small Austin because it was easier to get out of the former. But she had been driving when their car hit a lorry full of sand and they were both killed instantly. Fiona had been fond of her, but she could not understand anyone so utterly submerging her own personality.

Quentin wanted to know how these gentle people, absorbed in each other, had produced two sparks like Fiona and Lachlan. Fiona said they often asked themselves that. Lachlan's guess was that the family must be stronger genetically than they had believed. Something of this could be seen in the McDhuie portrait that hung above the fireplace. Said to be Hector, an early chief, her father had found it at a sale in Dingwall. The artist was unknown but the period was right. Hector's doublet and trews, checked with green and black, were designed to suggest tartan at the time when Highland dress was proscribed after the Rebellion. Quentin saw a likeness to Lachlan. Yes, she agreed, there was a resemblance, but her father always referred to Hector as wearing a Harlequin pantaloon. That was enough of the McDhuies. She had talked too much. She wanted to hear about Quentin.

He told her briefly of his parents, but he could not match her impulsive, revealing account. His father and mother had been affectionate and understanding, though they were not a closely-knit family. They had kept to themselves and did not impinge on each other. He valued his father's counsel, but he did not remember much in the way of emotional stress. That, Fiona rejoined, explained his reserve, the reserve he masked with his Donnish quips, his witty conceits.

'It's not so straightforward as that,' Quentin, shaken by her insight, protested. 'What you describe is probably due to Claude Albizzi's example. A veneer of facetiousness, and I promise you it's no more, is part of the currency in my new job.'

'So the merchant princes spend their time telling funny stories?' She made a face.

'I don't know how to say it, but an intense levity is very much the accepted thing. In the Square Mile, when we've finished our sums we have to convince our clients. That's not done by solemn advice, or a long tale of credits and debits. Claude's method is to lead them gently to see the folly of what they propose. Then they may look at it in a different light. On the first takeover bid in which I was involved we had to show the company directors that it was an illusion that they would add a new "dynamism" – that's the catchword – to the business they wanted to acquire. They had really been attracted by the prospect of increasing the size of their own company, of getting further up the batting order. The takeover wouldn't necessarily have improved their share earnings, but that was arguable. What we did was to draw a farcical projection of their staff insisting on promotion, higher salaries, status and perks. There would be no room in the car park for all their larger cars. There would be no money to pay for the petrol, and the dividend wouldn't be covered. Sounds absurd, but it allows time for second thoughts. The moral is that we're never more serious than when we're being facetious.'

76

'And were you being serious this afternoon, on the hill, when you said how much you'd enjoyed today?'

As he met the steady gaze of her deep brown eyes, he knew that she had meant what she'd said. He sensed too in her silence that his own feelings of attraction were returned, and he basked in the warmth that this knowledge brought him. He could not help contrasting her with other women he had known – all of them demanding, even predatory. Fiona, despite her generous instincts, her loyalties, her declared wish to preserve her independence, was strangely vulnerable. He could think of nothing better than to share his existence with the vibrant, sensitive figure opposite him. But he held back, because he knew already that to get involved would mean a permanent commitment. He could not bear to harm her with a casual affair, nor did he want that himself. But would he be justified in taking her away from her surroundings, from those who were closest to her, to a very different kind of life? He took refuge from his thoughts in another deliberate whimsy.

'Did you ever read a novel by Ian Hay, called "Pip"? he asked.

'What obscure joke is coming now?'

'I was given it at school. Even then it seemed dated, but there was a splendid conclusion. Pip, who has been pursuing his heroine without any success, enveigles her into agreeing that it should depend on a golf match between them.'

'And?'

'If I remember it aright, he wins on the last green. But only because she wants to lose.'

'Dear Quentin.' She moved quietly over and knelt by his chair. He leant forward and took her face in his hands, all his scruples forgotten. Her lips were cool as she returned his kiss.

'Dear, dear Quentin.' She laughed happily. 'Did you have to be so roundabout? I'm not a client.'

He kissed her again. They heard a car breaking on the gravel drive. He tried to hold her, but she disentangled herself from his grasp.

'No, not now. That's Lachlan. He'll be here in a minute. But you'll come back to Skye, won't you? I mean you haven't had enough of Old Portree and everything that goes with it?'

'I couldn't bear to miss the target a second time.'

'You won't.'

Part Two

Chapter VI

David McLeish, Fifteenth Laird of McLeish, a designation he
never affected and deprecated when others used it, was not
enjoying his breakfast. Pushing aside *The Times*, he took stock.
This was normally a process that afforded adequate grounds
for satisfaction. Item, he was fit. A weekly game of Real Tennis
at Lords and regular holidays in the Dordogne kept him active
and, as he was enviously assured, looking younger than his
years. He was prepared to concede an element of vanity, but
that was not a major blemish in his balance sheet. Only lunatics
did not inspect their reflection in the mirror.

Item, he was rich. He had achieved the habit of life he sought.
No bachelor could enjoy more elegant quarters than his set in
Albany. He had his books and a collection of modern paintings
carefully garnered at the more recherché sales. His housekeeper was efficient and unobtrusive and his cellar revealed a
catholic taste.

Item, he had a rewarding job in which, to use the great Cal-
vinist Reith's phrase, he was fully stretched. He had reor-
ganised U.W.P.'s overseas marketing. More recently he had
tested his standing on the Board with a proposal to set up the
Barley-corn Trust as an example of enlightened patronage.
Though he regarded most of his colleagues as philistines they
had agreed without argument that the Trust, intended to encourage rising artists, would be worth a modest outlay in order
to improve the company's public image. Before long he would

be Chairman of U.W.P. There was no fixed retiring age, but the present incumbent could not last long. The question was whether his doctor or his fellow Directors would ease him out of the Chair.

By now he had identified the irritation that spoiled his appetite for Cooper's Oxford Marmalade. Last night he had been cornered in the club by Archie Strathgarve. He was not alone in keeping his distance from Strathgarve who clung like a leech to anyone who would listen to him. Unkindly, but accurately, it was said he bored for Scotland. David could find no other members to rescue him, and Strathgarve was soon in voice about the day's debate in the Lords. It had been a bad day for the Highlands, he complained. Showed the country in an unattractive light. Impervious to David's lack of response, he recounted Their Lordships' reaction to the sad story of Aqua Tonica. Trouble started with Pontius Pilate, he said. David feared that this would be even more rambling and incoherent than usual. Pontius, Strathgarve continued, was born on the shores of Loch Tay. His mother was a Ballinluig woman and his father a Roman centurion. Had to do something in the long winter nights, Strathgarve chuckled lubriciously. What, asked David, had this to do with the Upper House? It appeared that the scion of a Scottish noble family had formed a company to make tonic water allegedly from an ancient recipe left by the Romans, called it Aqua Tonica, and put the head of the Procurator of Judaea on the label. He obtained a large Government subvention, built a factory on the Lochside, and for a time gave every sign of prospering. But as soon as the statutory period had expired, so that there was no obligation to repay the grant, he sold out to Associated Minerals. The English consortium, anxious to extinguish an opponent, closed down the factory and two hundred employees were made redundant without notice.

The gravamen of the charge against Aqua Tonica was that the whole exercise had been planned from the outset. They had stayed in business, with a great deal of attendant publicity, only long enough to provoke their long-established competitors into considering a takeover. Aqua Tonica had made a killing at the

82

expense of their employees' livelihood. Labour Peers had been quick to denounce this example of callous capitalism. What made it worse, according to Strathgarve, was that a native had dirtied his own doorstep.

'Cupidity is not confined to the Scots,' David was stung into replying.

'Damned shame, the whole affair. Couldn't you have intervened? They would have been just as willing to sell to you. It was the cash they wanted.'

'U.W.P. are not in the soft-drinks trade.'

'But you make gin as well as whisky. Would it not be worth your while to have your own tonic water? Think of these poor wretches, and their families, thrown on the dole.'

'We are not an employment agency. We stick to our own last.'

'And it gives the other side a stick to beat us with.'

'Politics are for our political masters, as they're amusingly called. Now, if you'll excuse me.'

Strathgarve was not to be so easily dismissed.

'I was over at The Keep last month. Your brother, and that bonny wife of his, are doing a fine job with the Estate.' A malevolent gleam appeared in his eye as he glared at David. 'A credit to your family.'

It was not the implied contrast between his refusal to contemplate saving Aqua Tonica and Charlie's obstinate efforts to maintain his patrimony that infuriated David. It was the reference to Kirsty.

Kirsty, his beautiful, desirable Kirsty. He did not think of her so often now, but the memory was suppressed, not erased. When she had married his brother, he had had to make a conscious effort not to be consumed by humiliating jealousy. He had no real animus against Charlie. He acquitted him of influencing their father's Will. That would have been too devious for him. But he despised the supine way in which he had subscribed to his father's outworn mythology, and his unqualified acceptance of the need to keep the whole tribal ritual in being. Nor could David condone someone giving up a promising, already distinguished, Army career to be a bonnet-laird in a peat-bog.

There was no reason why Charlie should not have aspired to Kirsty's hand. They had all been brought up together, and David could point to no prior claim. But that she should have discouraged, and eventually ignored his attentions in favour of his younger brother, that was what rankled. If he put their qualities, their powers of attraction, their prospects in the balance, he could not – however much he tried to be impartial – believe that Charlie had more to offer. The equation had, however, given him no comfort. David had arranged to be abroad when the marriage was celebrated in the High Kirk of St Giles.

Since then he had all but severed his links. He recalled his last communication when Charlie proposed to sell the Allan Ramsay paintings to pay for some ridiculous alterations to The Keep. He had thought of buying them himself as an investment, but that would have seemed to admit some vestigial interest. His solicitor, when instructed to convey his agreement to the sale in provocative terms, had protested. Why, he asked, spoil it with a jibe? He was being generous and it was a pity to be so gratuitously offensive. David had reminded his legal adviser that there was a latent war between him and the inhabitants of The Keep. In warfare, he understood, you turned everything to your own advantage. So he must remind them of his contempt for the feudal ideals they admired and cosseted. Besides, he added, to temper the solicitor's disapproval, if he did not strike an attitude and include an envoi like that they would think he was becoming fuddled with their beloved Scotch Mist.

If Kirsty had ceased to haunt his waking thoughts she had also spoiled him for anyone else. At the time of his rejection he had deliberately thrown all his energies into his own work. He had just joined U.W.P. and there was more than enough to engage his attention. Then he had begun to think he was overdoing it, like a disappointed Victorian suitor fleeing the country to hunt the White Rhino. With the passage of time he had been more at peace, though he seldom sought women's company. Till recently.

He realised with a shock that thinking of Kirsty had emphasised anew the difference between Bianca and all his other
friends. She came from a world foreign to his experience. Signorina Bianca Liberta (her real name was Montone) was the
latest luminary in Italian films. As such he would not have met
her. But she was also under contract to Aphrodite Products, the
cosmetic firm owned by U.W.P. Before David reached a position of authority in the company, U.W.P., in the fashion of the
time, started a policy of diversification. It did not work. Whisky
did not blend with foreign bodies. David had gradually persuaded the Board to dispose of their ill-sorted subsidiaries, and
only Aphrodite remained to spoil the symmetry of U.W.P.'s
assets. He was determined to get rid of it. Somewhat against the
odds he had carried the negotiations with the giant American
conglomerate, Sacher Inc., almost to the point of conclusion,
and Sam Sacher, the head of the Corporation, was expected in
London to settle the deal. David had learned that Sacher had
another connection with Signorina Liberta. One of his companies had put up part of the money for her latest film *Daughter
of Poppaea*, shortly to open in Britain.

Thinking he should inspect the goods he was proposing to
sell, David had attended Aphrodite's latest preview. There he
met Bianca. His equipoise was shattered. His rationale, his
ascetic self-discipline offered no protection. In his eyes she was,
quite simply, a goddess. He took her out to lunch, then to
dinner, and when she flew back to Rome it was with mutual
promises of a reunion as soon as she returned to London.

He rose from the breakfast table. She was due at Heathrow
this afternoon. He would ring her as soon as she reached the
Savoy. The picture of Kirsty was disappearing out of focus.

Fortunately for the preservation of sanity, no one can be at
both ends of the telephone at once. David would have needed all
his reserves of self-control if he had observed the scene when he
asked to speak to Bianca in the Savoy Grill Room.

'Signorina Liberta, there is a call for you. Will you take it at
your table?' The Head Waiter hovered respectfully with an

ivory receiver in his hand. Customers like the Italian film star and her escort, the Head of Sacher Inc., called for his personal attention.

'Yes, please.' Bianca withdrew her hand from beneath Sacher's.

'Hullo. Hullo, David. Thank you so much for the beautiful flowers. Yes, we were an hour late. I don't like your Trident. Tomorrow? Not for lunch, and I don't know about the evening.' She saw the frown gathering on her companion's face. It seemed to make up her mind. 'Yes, I think so. About eight-thirty. That will be heavenly.' She put the phone down. 'That', she said in reply to his raised eyebrow, 'was David McLeish.'

'The whisky man?'

'Meanwhile my boss until you absorb Aphro in your great empire.'

'I thought you were going to dine with me tomorrow.'

'You're not to monopolise me. You've had nearly all my time since I flew in this afternoon. Wait.' She held up a finger to stop his interruption. 'I've spoken to Mamma about you. I said you had designs on me.'

'For Christ's sake. Do we have to talk about your mother?' Sacher had no illusions about maternal influence when it came to putting Italian film stars under contract. When the promoters, parasites, and the taxmen had taken their cut, the mother was often the only one who benefited – much more than her daughter. The contract would state that Mamma was to be provided with food, accommodation and clothes in keeping with her status as the star's parent. Then Mamma, who until now had spent her time scrubbing and cooking, moved into the Excelsior Hotel. When not shopping in the Condotti or Via Veneto she consumed the mountains of pasta which a trolley regularly brought to her private suite. She had reached the promised land – till thrombosis rang down the curtain on the gluttonous spectacle. Bianca did not share the Neapolitan origins common to many of her profession. She came from a good family, but she was still much subject to 'Mammisma'. She had a vigilant and protective parent.

'You're a big girl now. Capable of taking your own decisions. You know I have the greatest respect for your mother. I hope you made clear that my proposition was an honourable one.'

'What a wonderful phrase! To be *la troisième Mme Sacher*? Mamma likes you, but she would rather not play bridge against you. She said you must be patient. Let's change the subject. When are you travelling to Edinburgh? Can I come in Hermes?' This was the fanciful name of Sacher's private jet.

'I haven't said I'm going.' His schedule was planned weeks ahead. It had not, till Bianca suggested it, included a visit to Edinburgh where *Daughter of Poppaea* was to have its world première at a Festival performance. But looking appreciatively at her slim figure outlined by the smoke-coloured chiffon he knew quite well that he intended to be there. He had made up his mind to marry her if he could not have her any other way. He was not used to being frustrated, least of all by an Italian matriarch.

'But you are.' She laid a hand on his wrist and looked at him from the depths of her dark eyes.

'We'll see. I can manage only one night.'

'Kind, generous Sam. I want you to be there. Not just for *Poppaea*, which you've seen many times. We're going to announce my next film. It's based on a romantic Scottish story.'

'The one about the two brothers? What's it called? *The Master of Ballantrae*, isn't it? I thought they hadn't decided on the leading man.'

'Mastroianni can't do it. I'm glad, because he'd have had the top billing. Paolo Paolino and Tom Savitz are going to be the male leads. I don't like Paolo. He's always sticking his fingers into me.'

'The dirty bastard.'

'Or trying. But he won't upstage me. Think how lucky I've been. They wanted Monica Vitti, then Diana Rigg, and they're both far better known than me. If it's a success . . .'

'Will you be satisfied?'

'I might be. Really I might, Sam.'

*   *   *

87

'Glad to have you back from the land of the mountain and the flood, Quentin. How do we stand on the whisky project?' Claude Albizzi asked.

'The figures are being checked. Meanwhile, a subjective impression. It's promising – with one or two provisos. Charlie McLeish runs his Estate, and the Distillery, with the utmost efficiency. So far, so good. But what inspires him is a fanatical desire to justify himself in the face of his brother's scornful disposition. It's ironic that David McLeish, who's a pretty cool customer anyhow, should be the No 2 at U.W.P. Charlie is more concerned to thumb his nose at him than to make money. From our point of view that's unsound.'

'I told you we were part-time psychiatrists.'

'There's also a heavy Gaelic cloud hanging over The Keep and its environs, but I suspect that's largely to prevent anyone from observing the natives too closely. What do we do now?'

'D. McLeish is the principal adversary, both from fraternal antipathy and because U.W.P. will oppose any change in the export regulations. Let's leave him to the end. You'll meet him anyhow at the Aphrodite wake. I want you to come and watch Sacher in action. Plenty of scrute, but still inscrutable. For the time being we'll see what support we can muster in the stews of Whitehall. You'll find that's enough to make mad the guilty and appal the free.'

'Does the Scottish Office come into this?'

'I'm not sure what locus they have, but it would do no harm to bowl one at their Minister of State. The Board of Trade certainly have an interest. The man to see is Paul Nollekens. He used to be at the F.O. but he's moved sideways and he's their mastermind on exports. I know him well enough to fix an appointment for you. Ca marche?'

'There's one thing that worries me. When I left The Keep I could not help noticing the damp marks that stained the stone façade despite Charlie's careful management. Then I saw an eagle soaring over Ben More. Like a baroque parody – the Castle of Otranto transplanted. Isn't Charlie a forlorn hope? He'll be outgunned by U.W.P.'s artillery.'

'That remains to be seen. We're professional advisers, not to be distracted by any Landseer setting.'

Quentin grinned. Despite his infectious flippancy, Claude never lost sight of his objective. Their exchange of views was stimulating, but it would have been easier to accept Claude's dictum if he had not spent a day on the hill with Fiona.

Chapter VII

The Scottish Office, its entrance dignified by a recessed carriage bay and a pillared portico, is arguably the handsomest of Government Departments. Originally a nobleman's town house, it is an unlikely setting for a hive of bureaucracy. Quentin admired the pargeted ceiling and the splendid proportions of the room when he was shown into the presence of the Right Honourable John Gardner, M.P., Minister of State.

'The most peaceful view in London.' Gardner pointed to the window. 'Look at that absurdly rural vista across the pond in St James's Park. The only drawback is that for two months in the year the Brigade of Guards rehearse Trooping the Colour outside. If we want to telephone, we have to go to the other side of the building to escape the military music.'

'There are still many who would be envious. I must say I'm very grateful to you for agreeing to see me at short notice. I know that, unlike Chaucer's scholar, Ministers are busier than they seem.' Quentin was amused to see that the Minister's bow implied his assent to this obvious sweetener.

'My Private Secretary', the Minister had a plummy voice, 'said it was about a development project in the Highlands.'

'Yes. If it proceeds it will double employment in the district.'

'Job opportunities. The new shibboleth. The public, Mr Lawrence, are convinced that we in Government are prepared to expend unlimited public funds to create job opportunities.

If a Minister may be forgiven a metaphor,' he continued complacently, 'every time I hear that word I think of a rabbit-warren. We assume that if we burrow enough holes the unemployed bunnies will obediently take one each, and everyone will be happy. But it doesn't work like that. I'm sorry. I interrupted.'

Quentin outlined Charlie McLeish's proposal and the difficulties caused by the three-year embargo. If it were lifted, there would be substantial new export business. He concluded with the hope that, as a desirable Scottish enterprise, the Ben More scheme would have the support of the Scottish Office.

'Unfortunately,' Gardner replied, 'it is not open to the Scottish Office to intervene. Whisky, believe it or not, comes within the province of the Minister of Agriculture, Fisheries, and Food. It counts as a food.'

'I hadn't thought of claiming nutritional advantages for our proposal.'

'The great Scottish public are blissfully unaware that their most famous product is dealt with by an English Minister. But the trade, led by U.W.P. and Distillers, are quite content that it should be so; and no one wants to make a fuss. If you want to argue about the export market, exports generally – including whisky – are for the Board of Trade. There it is. I regret there's not much that I can do for you.'

'I'm surprised', Quentin thought the Minister's disengagement was offensively glib, 'that you have no concern for a project that would clearly be beneficial, both to the national economy and to the inhabitants of an impoverished rural area. The least I would expect would be an endorsement that this was an idea which had some merit.'

'That would be prejudicial.' Plumminess made it sound ominous.

'I really don't follow.'

'Let me explain. A development on that scale would require planning permission.'

'I gather the planners say they would not have any objections.'

'Probably not. But that's only the beginning. The more logical, reasonable, and well designed your project is, the more likely it is to be fiercely opposed. As soon as your scheme is advertised – especially as it is intended to build in what has been designated as an area of outstanding scenic beauty – every hairy do-gooder, crank and vested interest in the country will lodge objections. Then there will have to be a tedious public inquiry and a report to the Secretary of State. So you can see that with this possibility in mind anything I said now could be regarded as prejudicing his statutory decision.'

'Amazing. There are some things that the Secretary of State can do?' Quentin asked sarcastically.

'We enjoy the reverse of the harlot's prerogative of power without responsibility. We have the responsibility – or at least most people think we have – for almost everything that happens in Scotland, but we have very little power to do anything about it. I would be prepared to elaborate on the allocation of Ministerial functions, but the present system has stood the test of time, and, of course' he added with a self-satisfied smile, 'it has the admirable consequence of making it unnecessary for Scottish Ministers to divert their attention to projects like your Distillery which have no electoral advantage.'

'What exactly do you see as the role, if any, of the Scottish Office?'

'We are essentially a suppliant department. We claim to speak for Scotland and we plead with our colleagues in other Ministries to lend a kindly ear to our supplications. Sometimes I think the set-up was devised by George Bernard Shaw as an intellectual conundrum.'

'To which you don't have the key?'

'No. That would be too much. In any event, let me add this. If I were to try to help you, it would mean going out on a limb, risking my reputation – for what it is worth.' A deprecatory gesture revealed his view that it was worth a great deal. 'Now, a prudent Minister when he is appointed will sit down and ask himself what the three things he most wants to do while in office are, and what he most wants to be remembered for, realising he'll be lucky if he achieves one of them. I'm afraid that on my reckoning the Ben More Distillery doesn't even get into the semi-final. But don't let me discourage you from trying the Board of Trade. As you will appreciate, I regard it as an indispensable part of my function to be accessible, and if I'm consulted I'll certainly do nothing to harm your cause. I suppose it would be impertinent of me to offer you a glass of whisky since I can give you nothing else. It wouldn't do to have you think we're inhospitable.'

Still taken aback by the Minister's effrontery, Quentin declined.

Unaware that his brother's standard had been raised in Whitehall the previous day, David was agreeably occupied.

A small adjustment of the pole, and the punt resumed its smooth progress upstream. Standing in the stern, shirt open at the neck, sleeves rolled up, he propelled the lazy craft with the same tenacity that he applied to the affairs of U.W.P. A slight breeze ruffled the water against the overhanging prow.

It was a good day, and nowhere on the Cam was there a more enchanting sight than Bianca, at ease on the cushions with her hand dipped in the water. Only his sense of the ridiculous worried him. There might be something banal in seeming to ape a scene from *Salad Days*, and he abhorred banality.

It had been a good day from the start. Saturday, he had assured her, could not be spent in London. He would take her to Cambridge, for the river if the weather was clement, for a visit to the colleges if it was not. A Fortnum's hamper in the boot, he drove into the courtyard of the Savoy.

'I adore the Rolls Royce,' she bubbled with excitement beside him as the grey-coated attendant tipped his hat, 'but I'm never allowed to sit in front. I have to lean forward in the back so that the photographers can see me. There's often a scuffle with the crowds round the car. All for publicity. In Rome it's sometimes necessary to have one's dress torn for the benefit of the reporters.'

'Good Lord!'

'Don't be so prudish.' Bianca was no deb fetched up for a May Ball. 'Anyhow, they're not new dresses. Mamma's very practical, and we have two huge Nubians who stand at the studio gates. I call them Ro and Re. They're great friends of mine. They keep the bottom-pinchers from getting too near. But you get used to it. You can get used to anything when you know it's only for a short time, before someone else takes your place as the next Star of the Century.'

Much of her conversation was in the same realistic vein. A film actress's career was brief, and illusory. There was nothing more artificial since the age of the Empress Poppaea, whose daughter she had played. She hoped she could reach her peak and escape before the shabbiness rubbed off on her.

'As much of a jungle as that?', he asked as they tied up for lunch.

'Unless you're fantastically lucky, your image soon dims.' She laughed. 'You can read the notices of your successor's first films, then you can begin to watch for another name on the dressing-room door. Or you can haunt the studios hoping for character parts. I don't intend to do that.'

'*Quant'è bella giovinezza.*' He poured a ready-mixed Martini from the flask.

'Very true. Make the most of it before the wrinkles appear. She sipped her drink. 'How delicious. Why did you bring me here?'

'I thought it would be a good setting for you.' This was true. With her long black hair and white summery dress she looked like a dark butterfly skimming the surface. 'Partly nostalgia as well. One is always tempted to go back.' This was not the whole explanation. David was admittedly happy to recall his time as an undergraduate. He had been unable to afford as much high living as he had wanted, and he had been stimulated by the hard thinking he had prescribed for himself. Cambridge had been a liberating experience. When he had rebuffed the suggestion that as a General's son he would want to join the O.T.C. he felt that for the first time he was free of the McLeish mystique. Prince Charles Edward had turned back at

94

Derby. More immediately – and this was the real reason for choosing today's expedition – the river carried no memories of Kirsty. 'But' he added wryly, 'middle-aged men shouldn't try to revisit the glimpses of the moon.'

'Now you're sorry for yourself. I'm not sorry for you. Everything you want is yours, isn't it? You're rich, and important. You have an exciting job, and a beautiful white Rolls Royce. What more could you ask for? Angular, stern David, why is there no Mrs David? I mean you're not a queer, and you don't go about making passes at everyone in reach. What is the dread secret?' She might have read his thoughts.

"Suppose we say I'm a perfectionist.'

'I'll have to think about that. The idea of perfection makes it a challenge. I'm supposed to start thinking how far I would meet the criterion, is that it?'

'The best thing Aphrodite did was to choose you as their symbol.' He held up the flask.

'I can't keep this up. I shouldn't have another Martini before lunch. But these are too good to miss. What do you think about my new part? Do you think I'll manage the heroine who has to choose between these two horrible brothers? One was the devil, literally, and the other a dull, drab *contadino*. She has a lot of thinking to do.'

'I don't know that Stevenson's heroine was greatly given to thought. The young Laird of Durrisdeer, whom she wants, goes off to the war. She marries the clottish younger brother. Then the wicked one returns from the dead and she's in trouble. I never thought her very interesting. The whole situation's too obvious and made too melodramatic. But I look forward to hearing your Scottish accent.'

'It may not be necessary. We're going to shoot most of it in Corsica, but they haven't decided whether it's to be a Corsican family feud, or a Scottish one. I think it will be Scottish. There's no advantage world-wide in being Corsican rather than coming from your country, don't you agree?'

'Probably – if that's the alternative.' He produced smoked salmon, cold grouse and salad, and opened a bottle of hock.

'I can't possibly eat all this. Which means I'm going to try, for once. You told me, rather reluctantly I thought, that you came from a Scottish Estate. Would it do for our location, for some of the scenes at least?'

'I think not. My brother and his family live there. It's their home. They wouldn't welcome intruders.'

'As short as that? He doesn't sound very friendly, or like his brother. Is he like you?'

'Not at all. We've gone entirely different ways. He seldom leaves Skye, and I haven't seen him for years.' David had not been in Skye since his mother died, and the recollection of her funeral still disturbed him. He was inescapably the Laird, but he would not be a guest in The Keep. Instead, he had spent the previous night in a comfortless hotel in Portree and left as soon as decency allowed. Charlie had made a pathetic attempt to behave as though there was nothing between them and had been distressed at his distant civility. He had brushed aside the offer to show him the improvements that had been made to the Estate, and seeing the unspoken reproach in Kirsty's face, he had given her no chance to speak to him alone.

'He's married?'

'Yes, with two sons.'

'So there wouldn't be a film about the Master of – where is it?'

'Borve, in the Island of Skye. No. No story, and no film.'

They dozed in the sun. Bianca slept. But David had misgivings. A recurring picture of himself as an ageing satyr needled him. That was not how he behaved. The quickness of her reactions as much as her brittle talk made him feel his years. Was it fair to court her as he was doing? Fairness did not enter into it. He was bemused by the aura that surrounded her. He took a second bottle from the cold box.

'I'm not allowed to get sunburnt.' She rubbed her eyes as she woke up.

'Too old for Ganymede, I'm afraid.' He felt like a veteran actor playing a juvenile lead. He filled her glass.

'But much more skilful. The pampered youth would have

96

made a mess of opening the wine. I choose experience.'

Reluctantly they repacked the hamper and headed downstream. 'You're a good *gondoliere*. You'd look well in the straw hat with the ribbons.'

'*Oè! Oè!*' He gave the pole a stronger thrust. 'I can't imitate their melancholy call. A sad place, Venice.'

'When you get the bill at the Danieli, it certainly is. But there's an air of mortality everywhere. I keep meeting the funeral gondola on its way to San Michele. We agree about the Serenissima.'

'Not only that.'

'I know what you're thinking. It's quite true. I feel I've known you for a very long time, that I know you better than I do.'

David was greatly encouraged by the tenor of the conversation. He wanted to pursue it, but the punt required too much attention, especially as they neared the more crowded reaches of the Backs.

'What a fascinating bridge.'

'Queens!' They drifted towards the bank as he replied. 'The story is that it was designed by Isaac Newton, and is so mathematically perfect that the wooden struts hold together without nails. I fear there's no truth in the legend. It was erected on a Chinese model when everything oriental was in vogue. It appears in contemporary prints.'

'It appears in contemporary prints,' she mocked him. 'What a dry, impersonal phrase. So like you. But I bow to the authoritative way you say it. That's part of your charm. No effort, and all the best lines given away. In Italy I've always suffered from people – usually the most dreadful people – trying to impose their authority and get me into bed. But with you it's different. Authority flows naturally from you. I think you're a timeless person. Does that make you blush?'

Chapter VIII

'Mr Lawrence. Claude Albizzi telephoned, so I know roughly what the object of your mission is. I gather that the inheritors of the Medici tradition have developed an interest in the commodity field, and in an exotic commodity at that. I'm rather surprised that the smooth rotation of the Albizzi wheels can produce anything so eccentric. Do speak.'

Sir Paul Nollekens, K.C.M.G., Second Secretary at the Board of Trade, paused. Quentin was conscious that it was a lacuna which he would have to fill with something equally oblique if he was to enlist the sympathy of the Mandarin opposite him. A courtier, he recalled, should be able to match his prince's mood. The figure opposite him was not princely, but he held the strings. Nollekens' bland smile concealed what his ultimate disposition might be. He was also a strangely pyramidal shape. The crown of his bald dome broadened to plump cheeks. His sloping shoulders gave way to the depth of a full belly beneath his watch chain. His arms resting on their elbows tapered to fingers delicately poised in a triangle whose peak supported his chins. Nollekens was built for defence in depth.

'I should explain that I've discussed this with the Scottish Office. I thought I could count on their support for something so obviously lucrative. The Minister assured me that although he is like Andromeda tied to the rocks – so far as overt approval is concerned – he would do nothing to hinder our progress.'

98

'Let us not lightly invoke the names of the anointed.' Nollekens looked piously at the ceiling. 'It is occasionally necessary to load the Ministerial cannons and wheel them out. Sometimes they even have to be fired at each other. But we're still a long way from lighting the touch in your case.' His smile was gently deprecatory.

'Then', Quentin sought to put him on the defensive, 'I would be disappointed to learn that you would not commend a scheme as logical as it is equitable.'

'My dear fellow,' Nollekens appeared to be enjoying the pavane, 'Logic and equity are not, I fear, personified at the Board of Trade. They are not, strictly speaking, relevant. That may sound depressing.'

'It's not exactly likely to raise a cheer.'

'If I may go further, our appointed task – at least in my humble opinion – is to refrain from intervening, unless there's a decisive argument for it. That means unless Ministers lose their nerve. If we do have to interfere, we should do no more than create the conditions where the good may prosper and the evil find some incidental obstacles to achieving their illegal aims. There's a mediaeval apothegm to the same effect, but the reference escapes me.' He contemplated the ceiling once more, seeking to conjure up the name of some obscure scholiast.

'On that basis you would justify an inequitable three-year rule?'

'All rules are inequitable, or may be so represented. But we can find good, pragmatic reasons for the present restrictions on exporting whisky before it is three years old.'

'I would be grateful if you would exemplify.'

'We are responsibly advised by the principal producers that the reputation of this great drink would suffer at once if it could be sold in a comparatively raw state. Can I invite you to regard it as an admirable symmetric syndrome?' He oozed confidence.

'Although these producers are very much an interested party.'

'Quite so. But the volume of our whisky sales overseas, and the effect on our balance of payments, is such that we have no practical alternative to accepting their advice.'

'My information is that you couldn't tell the difference between whiskies that were two, three, or five years old.'

'That may be so, but I can only ask you to accept my considered view that the effect on your palate is of no weight, no weight at all, compared with the pressure that can be brought by the large combines. Not to be mealy-mouthed, by U.W.P., and the other big boys.'

'I must defer to your experience, but it hardly seems fair. There must be some democratic process by which this, as it seems to me, totally unjust cartel can be exposed.'

'You can, I dare say, incite Members of Parliament to go through the ritual sequence of writing to the President, asking questions in the House, and raising adjournment debates. But even there you are up against two major obstacles.'

'Namely?'

'First, for a campaign of that kind to succeed, you have to enlist public, preferably vocal and vociferous, support. I submit, Mr Lawrence, you would find that extraordinarily difficult. Your plan has no public appeal. It won't bring down the price of whisky. And think of all the ignorant imbibers who imagine they've got a drop of the real stuff of such antiquity that it was probably bottled by Noah. They would be horrified to learn that it could be sold out of bond after two years. One's heart bleeds for them, it really does.' Nollekens enjoyed his histrionics.

'Surely a change would be popular in the Highlands, especially in Skye where it would bring more jobs?'

'There is only one other Distillery in Skye, so you needn't expect a gathering of the clans on that score. I must also remind you that the constituency circumstances are unfavourable. The sitting member is a Liberal, an excellent fellow, I believe. But you can judge for yourself whether either of the major parties would risk a row with the powerful interests involved in order to appease an out-of-the-way Liberal constituency. You can imagine how long it would take Ministers to count heads, to examine the entrails. They won't admit that in public, but it is regrettably true.'

'You depress me on all counts.'

'Let me add a postscript which might suggest that I know what I'm talking about – although that is a dangerous form of self-deception. You will be aware that whisky matures only when it is in the barrel. I understand that when it comes out of the still it is pure and potable, but it doesn't taste like whisky as we know it. Then when it is embarrelled, if I may use the term, it becomes fiery and quite undrinkable. Thereafter it starts to mature, a process that continues as long as it is in the cask. I suspect that the point at which it loses its fieriness, and begins to mellow, is dangerously near the expiry of two years.'

'Some foreign countries rely on an analyst's certificate, rather than on age.'

'That's up to them, but the danger still exists. In practice, most whisky is sold when it is at least seven years old, which also indicates that to lower the minimum to two would be to court disaster, or at any rate be perilous. Now that the sun is over the yardarm,' Nollekens rose from his desk twisting his watchchain, 'we can be deemed to be in the *crépuscule*. I wonder if I could offer you a glass of something appreciably older. We needn't argue about the excellence of this Glenmorangie.'

Further along the Embankment, no great distance from the human filing-cabinet that houses the Board of Trade, other libations were soon to be poured.

'It's not what you do do. It's more what you don't do.' Lena Horne's version of 'A new-fangled tango' was the last encore in her repertoire. The suggestive number was an old favourite with the Savoy audience and she spread her arms to acknowledge their prolonged applause. The dance floor, raised for the cabaret, descended hydraulically to its normal level and the first of the resident bands took up their instruments.

'Come on, let's dance.' Bianca led Sam Sacher from their table. While the young writhed frenetically and individually, many of those on the floor were of an age that still enjoyed bodily contact while in motion. Once again she found him an exciting partner. He was light on his feet and moved with an easy rhythm. More than that, he generated a magnetism that made her tingle. She did not resist when he held her closer.

'Not still sulking? It doesn't become you,' she teased him when the music stopped.

'I don't follow your reasoning, that's all.'

'I told you. The gossip columns strike a balance. They know I'm not worth as many carats as you. It's easy for them to decide that I'm after you. It does no harm for me to be seen with someone else.' This, Bianca knew, was disingenuous. She had asked David to escort her to a charity show the previous evening because she wanted to be with him. She enjoyed his company more each time she saw him. She was at once fascinated and frightened by his cool demeanour. His polite air as he guided her through the crowd at the cinema and the reception that followed had earned her admiration. He showed to advantage among the film moguls and their sycophants. But the chilly way he referred to his brother had alarmed her, the more since she felt drawn to his family by something that she could not identify. Meanwhile, Sam had his own vibrations.

'I'm flying back to the States the day after your Edinburgh première.'

'So soon?'

'I want you to come with me. We'll be married in New York. Go anwhere you like for our honeymoon. Then I'll open the Long Island house. You can redecorate it as you wish. I'll guarantee not to interfere with filming.'

'We will, of course, be in touch at all times with Sacher Incorporated, special telephone exchanges, or will radio stations be set up for the purpose?'

'Sometimes. World business doesn't stop even for our marriage.'

'And you must watch your famous percentage point. Don't you see my problem? Even if you can order more champagne by moving your left eyebrow, as you've just done!'

'Frankly, no.'

'Oh, Sam! I'll try to explain. Is that story about you and the

102

King of Sweden true?' The myth was that Sacher, who was accustomed to carry on his more personal correspondence by telegram, had dictated one to his friend the King of Sweden, inviting him to open a new Sacher plant. When he gave the address as Copenhagen, his secretary with unusual daring had remarked that His Majesty was more likely to be found in Stockholm. Sacher replied irritably that all these damned monarchs knew each other anyhow.

'No. That's bugged me for years. I told her not to bother me with the details.'

'But it could have been true. Everyone believes it. I don't want to be wrapped up in a cable and fired across the Atlantic just as you despatch messages to the Shah of Persia. A piece of paper to be read once and thrown in the wastepaper basket.'

'You exaggerate, my dear. You always do when you're wrong.' He grinned. 'You'd never find yourself in the garbage can.'

'I'm a European. I've no wish to live on the other side.'

'I know you're part English. You were at school in Switzerland. But you're more than that. You're international. That means you must feel the pull, the excitement of the States. Have you ever thought how many of the Heads of American Corporations are no more than second-generation immigrants? They haven't forgotten they came from Europe. They never do. Why, then, do they linger in Manhattan? Because that's where the real action is. Fission and fusion. All the elements, all the constructive ideas are there.'

'Sam, that's really very eloquent. I like you best when you become animated.' His diction became more staccato on the very odd occasion when he allowed his feelings to get the better of him. 'But it's frightening. That nuclear stuff would be too much for me. I'd get burnt at the edges – and none of Sacher's special creams would cure a singed skin.'

'I hope you'll think again, my sweet. Hermes will be empty flying off without you. But it will also leave you in a vacuum, if you stay behind.'

The moral which Bianca had drawn from Sam's account of

his Babylonian existence in New York would hardly have pleased him. Sam lived on power, untrammelled power which grew under its own momentum, power which would eventually claim its victims. David McLeish's authority was personal. But it was not intrusive. It would not prevent her from making the most of her private life and her public career. She intended to exploit both.

'A good job I didn't have Charlie with me. He'd have exploded.' Quentin was deploring the negative outcome of his assault on Whitehall.

'Perhaps a detonation was needed,' Claude Albizzi replied. 'But I know what you mean. Charlie sounds a trifle innocent to be let loose among *les bureaux.*'

'What with a Minister who uses office to inflate his ego, and the sapient Nollekens who is resigned to the inadequacies of the machinery and will do nothing about it, between them they have perfected a system that ensures total obstruction.'

'Agreed. Complete occlusion unless you can take them from the flank. But the two jokers you met are not the worst. There's a fellow at the Ministry of Education – M. T. Bladder is the appropriate name – who has been heard to say that nothing should be done that has not been done before, and that's not a caricature. He really means it. Your two are routine Government targets. We'll make no progress head on. The only way is to undermine their advisers, chisel at the supporting edifice.'

'Meaning U.W.P. It depends, as we thought, on David McLeish.'

'That won't be easy. There's an unholy alliance, or truce if you like, between Departments and the big Corporations. The most powerful can still avoid the mortmain of state interference. The multinationals – Sacher, for example – go their own way. If there's a local currency crisis they just switch their finances to another country. Even U.W.P. are safe from the clammy hand of Government – apart from their annual bleating about excise duty.'

'So we're farting against thunder?'

'There's a built-in bias against the small company. Dividends pegged in the sacred name of social justice, and ham-fisted regulations that change after each General Election. As long as we're in business we've got to help the poor little acorns. Some of them will become oaks. Of course we make far more out of large dealings for the blue chips, but we can discriminate occasionally.'

'I share the Albizzi tendency to favour the up-and-coming.' Claude's determination to stick to his beliefs, to stay untarnished by the shabby machinations he met, was what impressed him.

'Even so, Ben More is the double bugger. We'll try brother David, but I don't think it will work. If he says no, we're stymied. We had better prepare Charlie for a *non possumus* on his great scheme. We could find the money for a modest expansion. That's his best course, but it won't satisfy him.'

'He won't be dancing a Scottische in The Keep.'

'By way of contrast, I want you to come to Sam Sacher's jamboree tomorrow. As his merchant bankers, we're invited to a meeting of his European Board. David McLeish will be there to mark the absorption of Aphrodite. There's a party afterwards and you can exchange the first whiff of grapeshot. Meanwhile, there's a call from Skye for you. They want you to ring back. Better put on your glancing helm!'

'McDhuie House, Good morning.' The number was not Charlie's, and Quentin had wondered about its significance.

'Is that Fiona?' He thought he recognised the voice, although the line was bad.

'Quentin, I'm so glad you rang. We'll have to be discreet.'

'Not only humans have ears. Trouble at mill?'

' 'Fraid so. The atmosphere is curdly. There are two reasons. One leads to another and I'll have to be careful. If you remember our conversation at lunchtime on the hill, there's been a misfire. Do you follow?'

'Little Moses was found in a stream. Now Old Pharoah's daughter goes down to the water, and finds nothing left in that stream.'

'Very theatrical. Up and away. But too late. Inevitably the châtelaine took charge.'

'Inevitably would be right.'

'Now she knows, or at least I think so, and compassion's a great thing with her. This leads to the second reason. Whether or not there's been a row, there has been a physical tremor. Not said to be serious. Laughed off as nothing to worry about, but it would upset the insurance premium. Is all this too abominably mysterious? It's not easy for me to be so cryptic.'

'I think I've got it.' Quentin surmised that Morag had suffered a miscarriage. Kirsty had been involved, might even have driven her to the hospital at Portree, and had learned enough to make her suspect that Charlie was responsible. From that thought, and this would be in character, Kirsty was disposed to be forgiving. This might be as hard for Charlie to bear as the upbraiding he deserved. It was not certain what had taken place between the McLeishes, but in the upshot Charlie had experienced a minor heart attack.

'I wanted to speak to you,' Fiona went on, 'because if your news is what I suspect it's going to be you'll need to be very careful. Everyone's very brittle at the moment.'

'What a great gift you Gaels have for tearing each other's heart-strings. I'll be as gentle as any cooing dove. Have you shot any good stags recently?'

'I've had one more day out with Angus. We got two, one at Callum's Point.'

'I wish I'd been there.' Quentin had more than stalking in mind.

'So do I. It seems a long time ago. You've to come back. No excuses. I'm going to ring off before you make any.'

'Hullo. Hullo.' The line was dead. He thought of Fiona swaying towards him in her apricot dress, or crawling on all fours through the braken. He could smell her rough pullover as they crouched together among the rocks. She was a distraction he had not bargained for. Not in the Albizzi terms of reference.

Thoroughly baffled, he reopened the Whisky file, now bulging with analyses and accountant's comments. McLeish, C. *versus* McLeish, D. One man against an entrenched monopoly. A fight where one contestant held the commanding heights. There could be only one answer. Even the acknowledged Albizzi expertise seemed impotent. Pride, as Claude would say, was a bad word and there was plenty of it at The Keep, but Quentin wanted to go back to Skye a winner.

He closed the file. Further calculations would bring no profit. The figures were irrelevant in the face of Whitehall's obduracy. An equally irrelevant thought struck him. It was fortunate he was a merchant banker, not a doctor. The newspapers were full of a lurid case where the General Medical Council had expelled a practitioner for demonstrating his affection for a patient. He was not subject to the same restraint.

Chapter IX

David had done his homework on Sam Sacher when it became clear that he was seriously interested in acquiring Aphrodite Products. The preliminary discussion had been with Albizzi who spoke much the same idiom as U.W.P., and the negotiations had gone smoothly. There had been only a single session with the head of Sacher Inc. Sacher had eventually said he was satisfied with the terms but, much to David's surprise, had added the rider that the agreement could not be signed until it was approved by his European Board. This was an essential stage in the Sacher process, and David was invited to attend the ratification ceremony.

He looked forward to today's meeting. It would mark U.W.P.'s final disengagement from cosmetics, and once he reached the Chair there would be no more ill-conceived sorties into matters that were not the proper concern of whisky producers. Bianca's contract with Aphro would pass to Sacher Inc. but it had not long to run, and he had other plans for her. As he was received at the marble entrance of Sacher's London headquarters he rehearsed the salient points that had come to light about the boss man.

The growth of Sacher Inc. under Sam's direction had been impressive. Inheriting a cosmetic firm from his father, an Austrian chemist who emigrated to the States in the twenties, he had swallowed many of his rivals and made it the largest manufacturer of beauty products on either side of the Atlantic. In the last decade the Corporation had expanded rapidly into other fields – property, hotels, engineering and films, to become one of the leading conglomerates. There had been hard words about the earlier Sacher's Fascist connections – one of the benefits of having factories in Spain was that strikers could be thrown into jail – but his son had confined himself to financial and legal pressure on his competitors.

Sam's private life had been very public. His wives had been heritable assets. His first spouse was a blue-blooded neighbour from Long Island who did not like being an appendix to the annual accounts and took off with a golf professional. Her successor was the daughter of Palladian Hotels, one of Sam's more spectacular acquisitions. The marriage consummated the takeover. She sued him for mental cruelty and settled for record alimony. Nothing much there, no more than the normal sexual insecurity of the tycoon.

David was much more interested in an aspect of Sam's technique which he had detected at their first encounter – his obsession with figures. Sam had invented the theory of the percentage point. Any idiot could earn the initial dividend, say 10 per cent, but Sacher men had to make the 10 per cent into 10·9 per cent and keep the decimal advance going. All Sacher's costs, forecasts and results were fed into Zeus, his master computer. Zeus, he had assured David, could eliminate all human errors and reduce the Corporation's activities to numerical symbols. As he continued this dissertation it began to appear that figures, not words, were emerging from his lips. His head and shoulders assumed a square shape; lights flashed from the recesses of his eyes; it was a robot that was speaking. There was something unnatural in this excessive numeracy. It might, however, mask the absence of any original talent. This could be Sacher's Achilles heel. Sacher Inc. were not notorious for developing new ideas, or products. The emphasis had been on buying established firms, reshaping them, and feeding them into Zeus's insatiable maw.

Today, however, David was intent on examining how Sacher's hierarchy worked – a matter of more immediate concern. There were hierarchies and hierarchies. There was the feudal one based on inheritance, tradition and sentiment, to which his brother adhered. This had long been discarded. There was U.W.P., whose organisation had evolved as the company grew. This he would change. He disliked the U.W.P. system of appointing to the Board veterans who had spent most of their careers promoting their own brand – and sampling it so consistently that their glazed faces shone in the dark. He would replace them by a functional Board, a Board with clearly defined tasks that would fortify him in the exercise of the Chairman's power. But he would see how Sacher Inc. operated. He had reached the seventh floor.

'There's our man.' Claude Albizzi and Quentin saw David being shown to a seat further along the front row. Facing a raised dais, chairs were deployed in concentric crescents. Each was placed at an individual curved table wih its own microphone, and a place card indicating the name of the occupant. Television screens sprouted like fungi in the aisles. Solemn-faced Sacher men already filled most of the stalls. There was an atmosphere of uneasy expectancy.

'Christ!', muttered Quentin, 'should we not have taken our shoes off when we entered the shrine? Do they canonise by computer? What they need is a blast of Charlie McLeish on the pipes.' Instead of answering, Claude nodded towards the podium where Sacher was taking his seat, flanked by Barney Houlihan his Vice Chairman, and the Head of the European Board.

'Gentlemen.' Sacher's voice silenced the assembly. One of their number strode forward to a lectern. Opening his folder he began to intone the assets and liabilities of Aphrodite. While he spoke, his words were converted into figures and arrows on the television screens. His voice rose gradually till he reached his peroration, an estimate of profits over the next five years. There followed a passage of rigorous questioning as Sacher men in turn tested the accounts, the assumptions and conclusions. It was a formidable performance, the devotees worshipping at the altar of the percentage point. Sacher for the most part remained impassive, swivelling in his chair to study the demeanour of the speakers. The questions became more perfunctory. The sands in the hour-glass ran out. Sacher spoke: 'Aphrodite is incorporated.' The exorcism was over.

Quentin, bemused by the theatrical nature of the inquisition, glanced sideways at Claude's doodling. He had sketched a chimera-like figure. The goat had the legendary serpent's tail. But in place of the lion's head the drawing was rounded off with an accurate likeness of Sacher's more simian features. A chimera who knew what he was doing.

The doors at the back of the room slid silently apart, revealing detachments of waiters bearing drinks. Sacher men in a state of administrative ecstasy staggered towards them.

'This', said Claude, 'is much better than I.B.M. When Tom Watson, their original guru, was alive they had to drink tea. But Sacher likes his cohorts to enjoy themselves.'

'Champagne, Sir, Dry Martini, or Claverhouse Cream – a special whisky with the compliments of U.W.P.'

'That must be David McLeish's doing.' They helped themselves to Scotch. 'Let's make our number with him.'

'Quentin Lawrence', David acknowledged their greeting. 'I wondered if we'd meet when I heard you had joined Claude.'

'A sensitive touch.' Quentin tapped his glass. 'Yours, I imagine.'

'Call it a final offering to Zeus. A thankful one.'

'I thought it was an agreed sale between a willing seller and a willing buyer?'

'It was. Cosmetics are not really our thing. I hope Cluade will agree we weren't too difficult about terms. But as time went on I was afraid the entire equity of U.W.P. was going to be sucked into the giant computer.'

'I can well believe it after hearing today's Sermon on the Mount. Talking of whisky, I want to come and see you.'

'Albizzi concerned with wines and spirits?'

'One in particular. Old Portree.' Quentin saw a slight flickering of the eyelids.

111

'How curious. Too small for you, surely.'

'Can I come and talk to you about their worries?'

'Well . . .' He seemed to hesitate. 'Come anyhow. It's a long time since we had a talk. Would you ring my secretary? I'd better make my obeisances to our host.' He slipped through the crowd.

'Not exactly keen, old boy,' Claude commented.

'But not an outright refusal.'

'I doubt if he'd have agreed to see anyone but you. The main thing is that you've got your entrée, and that's really why you're here.'

They gazed with impersonal interest at the Sacher entourage obediently sipping their drinks as though they were chemical mixtures in test-tubes. Claude stopped the sacrificial victim who had been cross-examined throughout the afternoon.

'Congratulations on your presenation and on your stamina. As an outsider, I was most impressed.'

'You're very kind, Sir.' He snatched a glass from a passing tray. 'To make the presentation is a privilege, yes a privilege, with us. But', he took a large gulp, evidently in need of a stimulant,' do you know, I can't remember what day it is, far less the time?' He had the expression of someone who had seen Hamlet's father.

'Would you answer a question, if you have not expunged it all from your mind,' Quentin asked.

'At your service, sir.'

'Raw materials for talc. What is talc made from?'

'Principally Fuller's Earth, or diatomite.'

'In your speech you said they were in short supply?'

'Diatomite is, particularly in Europe. Why do you ask?'

'Curiosity, that's all. Thank you.' Quentin had a sudden vision of a Highland Loch. It was just conceivable that he might not be wasting his time. Claude had reminded him more than once that the most spectacular deals were often sparked off by a casual remark.

'I've just caught Barney Houlihan's eye.' Claude interrupted his thoughts. 'I want you to meet the Great Man before we go.'

Sacher broke off his conversaion as he saw them approach.

'Ah, Mr Albizzi. Are you satisfied that your advice was good?'

'Confirmed by your relentless electronics. In any event, if I had been wrong it would have been academic by now. Can I introduce my colleague, Quentin Lawrence?'

While they exchanged pleasantries Quentin's impression of the Chairman changed. The stern concentration, the overt reliance on the computer, was replaced by an easy informality. The waxen features came alive. His hands gesticulated in approval at one of Claude's witticisms. His eyes twinkled. Quentin was reminded of Til Eulenspiegel. The heretical thought occurred to him that Samuel Sacher might be having sport with his audience. Sacher was the self-confessed apostle of action. Had he construed the verb to act in two senses which combined in a single bravura performance? In that event its significance had been lost. No one cocooned, like Sam, in awed respect was expected to be funny, even momentarily.

'Mr Sacher, I understand you're interested in diatomite?' There was nothing to lose by pressing his hunch a little further.

'So?'

'Something in the main speech this afternoon.'

'You were listening, then? I observed Mr Albizzi was occupied with his drawing.' The grin took the edge off his riposte.

'I believe I know where there's a large natural deposit.'

'In this country? Is it on the market?'

'Yes. It could be.'

'You interest me. I fly to Brussels tomorrow. Back here before I go to Edinburgh. Then to New York at the end of the week. Would you be good enough to let Barney have such details as you're prepared to release?'

Chapter X

'Quentin, how many years is it since we last met – apart from Sacher's party?' David McLeish, at ease behind the elegant *bureau plat* that served as his desk, enquired affably.

'More than I care to remember. But you wear well, if I may say so.'

'One has one's code – although I sometimes feel that I'm in the sere and yellow leaf. What exactly made you join Albizzi?' There was no change in his voice. The switch to another subject had been so smooth as to be almost imperceptible.

'The groves of Academe were too constricting. You lose touch with reality. The gap between you and the undergraduate stretches. It begins to yawn and so do you. Claude had a vacancy, and it seemed worth a shot to get nearer the seat of power and see how the economy is manipulated. But after watching Sacher in action, perhaps I should go back to Renaissance studies. I was afraid we were all about to be programmed.'

'What I find odd', David nodded in agreement, 'is that he looks like a monkey, but monkeys should chatter: he doesn't. He opines – but very seldom. That exhibition we saw was all showmanship. The footlights and the orchestra may have been missing, but the actors were in the stalls. His European Board – as he calls it – are all men of straw. Their questions were not genuine: they were to reassure their Leader that they were loyal in their bondage. I had hoped to learn how his great,

114

omniverous empire worked, but there is nothing there apart from the inhuman Sacher playing his giant fruit-machine.'

That, thought Quentin, could be a serious misjudgment. It was belied by Sam's lively conversation in private and the shrewd lines that appeared on his face when he was interested in a new subject.

'Thank heaven', David went serenely on, 'U.W.P. is not like that. We have no difficulty in convincing our staff that we're selling man's noblest product, and they don't need carefully staged bouts of public flagellation to maintain our dividend. The problem is rather to protect ourselves against imitations and inferior spirits.'

The discussion was developing on ground of David's choosing. Feeling at a disadvantage, Quentin plunged in.

'I mentioned we've been consulted about your brother's Distillery.'

'I can't see why that should interest me.' The reply was level enough, but his expression hardened.

'Briefly, he wants to expand, add another still, and bottle under his own name.'

'I would not pretend that it's our policy to encourage small, independent producers. He'll find it hard-going.'

'It would be infinitely easier if the three-year ban was reduced to two.'

'Which, as you know, is contrary to Government regulations.'

'Which, as you know, depend largely on you and Distillers.'

'Not a chance of our supporting a change.' He shook his head. 'Our sales, I'm glad to say, rise by about 8 per cent a year in volume. The figures are readily available. This happy state of affairs requires one thing – confidence in our labels. We're not protected by an *Appellation Contrôlée*, like the wine trade, but all our responsible customers know they can rely on our not selling them a raw spirit. This would be jeopardised if a younger whisky could be exported. I don't believe', he continued blandly, 'you have any arguments, based as they are on a single Distillery, that would justify a change. The Board of Trade won't listen to any proposals, to let two-year stuff go for export. If I'm asked I will advise strongly against it.'

'I'm disappointed to find such rigid orthodoxy.' David's views coincided too completely with those of the egregious Nollekens in Whitehall to leave much room for hope. He paraded his, by now familiar arguments, but made no progress. He tried a different tack. 'Can I suggest an alternative, one we've not discussed with your brother? It's very much a second-best, but accepting for the moment that the embargo stays, and that plans to export a new blend are knocked on the head, what would be your reaction if he stepped up production of pure malt, I mean a substantial increase? Would U.W.P. take it?'

'That would not be my decision. Let's be clear about this. Your new proposal is that Ben More should make far more Old Portree for use in blending. We've been blending since 1860. Since then we've acquired some modest expertise. The art – and this applies to all the proprietary brands – is to balance the heavier Highland malts against those from the Lowlands which are lighter, and against grain whiskies. In passing, grain whisky isn't made in the original pot still – like Old Portree – but by a different process called after an exciseman named Coffey, who surely found the safest passport to immortality. Do I bore you?' There was something offensive about his effortless mastery of the facts.

'Far from it.' Quentin listened attentively for a fallacy onto which he could fasten.

'There are more than two hundred Distilleries in Scotland. There they are on the map.' He used the ornamental dirk from his desk to point to the flags on the chart that hung on the wall.

'Like a healthy rash of measles.'

'Quite. From these producers, about forty single whiskies go into each blend. The large companies undertake half a dozen blends in a week, so they've got to be able to count a steady supply from the warehouses. We have our own Distilleries, and we take very little from outsiders. Now we come to the blend itself. All right so far?'

'Admirably clear.' No doubt there was a hammer blow

coming to pulverise Old Portree's chances, but it had not arrived yet.

'The blender is the key man. He works in a laboratory – not a tarted up Highland bothy. He's a combination of chemist and artist. He assembles the blends according to his own recipe. He tests each individual whisky by 'nosing' – never drinking – it in the glass. If he's doubtful he rubs some on the palms of his hands, cups them round his nose, and sniffs. It all depends on the blender's nasal organ. To keep it in good working order he can't smoke or drink while at work. Once the blender has passed a whisky as suitable it is put into the Blending Vat where it is allowed to marry with the other constituents in the blend for at least six months. Then it is ready for bottling. Now', the dirk was pointed at Quentin, 'you see how a blender would react if he was suddenly told to take a whacking great load of Old Portree. His professional pride would be outraged. He would reject it, or accept only derisory amounts. I'm afraid we're very much in the blender's hands. What's more, Old Portree has a heavy, peaty flavour, not by any means to everyone's taste. Wait.' Quentin, seeing no useful purpose in continuing the discussion, which had become a monologue, had made to rise. 'The blends are, as I said, secret recipes, but they're changing all the time. If you compare today's whisky with the same brand prewar – should you be able to obtain a bottle – you'd find that it is much lighter.'

'I've noticed the lighter shade.' Quentin did not appreciate the point of the comparison.

'It's not the colour that counts. That can easily be adjusted – but don't believe all you hear about us using prune juice to give an impression of antiquity. It's the taste. As more women drink whisky nowadays, and adulterate it with ginger ale or even with lemonade, this trend will continue. So my view would be that the prospects of any blender taking a vast amount of Old Portree are simply not good enough to justify the capital investment required.'

'I have to put this to you.' Quentin found David's suave logic increasingly irritating. 'I'm only an intermediary, but I've stayed at The Keep.'

'And you were bewitched by the Misty Isle?' His smile carried no cordiality.

'I found much to admire.'

'And Charlie beguiled you with the Highlander's three basic rights – to take a salmon from the river, a deer from the hill, and make his own dram. I would have thought someone of your academic brilliance would have seen that sentimental twaddle for what it is.'

'Hardly.' Quentin had enjoyed his experience of the first two and he was not to be diverted from his argument. 'I've visited the Distillery with your brother,' he continued coldly. 'I would not be doing my job if I omitted to ask whether your attitude to expanding production of Old Portree is not – to be blunt about it – due to personal animosity.'

'I recognise your difficulty.' He looked at Quentin over his interlocked fingers. 'Please don't feel embarrassed. The answer is that it doesn't make a scrap of difference who owns the Distillery. My view is an objective one. I rather pride myself on cultivating objectivity. I can see from your face you're not convinced. But you and I are not going to quarrel over this. You'll accept a glass of Claverhouse Cream to mark our meeting after so many years.'

'You're too kind.' Quentin was not being sarcastic. He was reflecting that in both his attempts to enlist Government Departments to Charlie's cause, his adversaries had tried to assuage his disappointment with the soothing spirit. A third offer was apparently consistent with the pattern.

'This', David poured from the crystal decanter, 'is how to tell whether a blend has real quality. A little in the glass. Warm the edge with your hand. Chase the whisky gently round the glass to allow the bouquet to reach you. Sip it and roll it round the palate. If it has a harsh or sharp taste – which I hope this hasn't – there's too much grain.'

'You're not serious?' Self-parody was surely foreign to David's character.

'Of course. You were always too sceptical, my dear Quentin.'

Quentin walked slowly back to the Albizzi office. There had been no surprise in the cold, unyielding rebuttal. The arguments were those he would have used in David's place, although he would not have adopted the same arid, impersonal manner. It was the manner, more than what was said, that annoyed him.

An Oxford friend had once recounted the Warden of Wadham's phrase to describe an event, say a success in Greats or election to a Fellowship, which was likely to arouse jealousy. It would, he said, 'cause pain'. That was it. David had a gift for causing pain, courteously and confidently. Quentin had spared Charlie the anguish of a personal confrontation. He had achieved no more. Whisky had gone sour on him. A pity, because a Whisky Sour had been his favourite aperitif. The next one would taste too acid.

Seeing his reflection in a shop window, he squared his shoulders. He had looked despondent. But diatomite was still to be explored. If there really was a substantial deposit on the bed of Loch Dhuie, Charlie could make enough to compensate for the failure of the Old Portree project. Fiona would also benefit, and that had its own, private, importance. The prospect of selling to Sacher must be resolutely pursued. There was, however, the hellish question whether David could scupper the sale under the terms of his father's Will.

He put through a call to Albizzi's solicitor. Could he say whether legacy provisions applying to land and buildings would automatically extend to rights in minerals that might lie under the land, or more precisely under the water? No. The solicitor could not say off-hand. He wouldn't like to hazard any advice till he had seen the Will. Where were the minerals? In Scotland? In that case he certainly couldn't advise. The Scots had their own barbarous legal system.

Quentin was still thinking of tactics when he let himself into his flat. Absentmindedly he leafed through the pile of letters waiting for him. Circulars; one from his mother asking about

119

her investments, whose diminishing dividends worried her; one from his college. He sat down to read it. The Classical Tutor wanted help to complete his work on Angelo Poliziano, the scholar and intimate of the Medici family. He was happy with his study of Poliziano's writing in Latin and Greek, but a section on his poems in the Tuscan tongue and his part in Florentine politics would made it a definitive work. Quentin was an expert on Lorenzo de' Medici. Would he find it of interest?

He poured a whisky – after David's remarks he looked more carefully at the label – and reread the letter. It was an attractive proposal. A few months ago he would have agreed without hesitation. A critique of Poliziano's poems, both the ribald verses and the Spenserian *Stanze* would not be difficult, but there were others who could do it. The ambience of the Medici court was what had fascinated him. He believed that although the Medici had become demoralised by their own power, this had not prevented Il Magnifico from being the true embodiment of Renaissance man. Now it seemed a remote, irrelevant exercise. He was in daily touch with the modern equivalents of the fifteenth-century rulers. He had seen the pompous Minister of State corrupted by power he thought he had but could not wield. Nollekens was possessed of authority he had no intention of using. And there were the McLeishes: David who had changed his birthright for big business; Charlie finding that feudalism was not enough. They challenged him to find his own solution without becoming infected – if that was not too self-important. He knew what he had to do.

Turning over the page, he found a postscript. He could have dining rights and a room in college, perhaps at weekends, which he might find a gracious contrast to a self-service flat in Holland Park. Very true. But it was not enough. To accept the offer would mean that he was at best a dilletante banker. He could not agree to that. In his involvement with Albizzi he had already lost his amateur status. He laughed. Lorenzo was a famous falconer, but he had not tried stalking at Borve.

Sacher Inc. worked smoothly, inexorably, and with compelling efficiency. This Quentin had seen at first hand. One of the Corporation's remaining characteristics, as he was soon to discover, was a capacity to move with alarming speed, particularly when the Chairman was himself involved.

A brisk call from Houlihan confirmed that Sacher Inc. would be extremely interested in exploring the purchase of diatomite in the Island of Skye. He hoped they would be able to reach agreement about terms without any protracted argument. Sacher would look to Albizzi for advice on the kind of offer that would be acceptable to the owner, and the Chairman would like to see initial heads of a contract before he left for the States. When Quentin enquired if it was normal to proceed at this breakneck speed, there was a curious pause at the other end of the line. Houlihan said that if he appeared to hesitate it was because that question had not been asked before. It was no more than the customary rate which was taken for granted within Sacher Inc. It might be slower than usual since the Chairman was in festive mood and had not asked for the computerisation within hours.

Quentin observed that an immediate conflict of interest arose. (This was a point that had been worrying him.) While Albizzi acted for Sacher, they had also been consulted in another connection by one of the diatomite owners. There could be embarrassment, if not impropriety, if Albizzi were to advise both sides. This did not impress Houlihan who retorted abrasively that it was Quentin who had first raised the matter. He suggested that Sacher should make available to Albizzi their data about world prices, likely cost of extraction and other relevant considerations. It would then be open to Quentin to draw up an objective memorandum. Seeing that he was about to be engulfed by a large Sacher wave before he could draw breath, Quentin asked for time to consult his principals in Skye who had not so far been brought into the picture. Houlihan sounded unhappy at the prospect of any kind of intermission and said he would ring again later in the afternoon.

His second call followed so quickly that Quentin suspected

he had just had time to report to, and take instructions from, the Ancient of Days. Mr Sacher, he said, fully appreciated Quentin's problem. He thought, however, that his difficulty of acting for both parties could be turned to advantage at a round-the-table discussion. Since time was short, Mr Sacher would be grateful if Quentin and the owners from Skye could meet him in Edinburgh on Friday. Transport from London in his private aircraft, and accommodation, would be provided, and Mr Sacher would like everyone to regard themselves as his guests. Quentin could think of no reason for not accepting this Imperial offer – if a stronger word were not appropriate – and agreed to transmit the invitation to Skye. Houlihan added that they would all be invited to attend the *Daughter of Poppaea* reception. On this generous, but incongruous note, Houlihan signed off with the expectation that they would meet at the airport. Meanwhile, Quentin had to break the news to The Keep.

'Hullo, Kirsty. This is Quentin. How are things at the ranch?'

'Quentin, how lovely to hear you. We're all well.' Her voice took on a more guarded tone. 'At least nearly all well. Charlie's had a fright, but he's better. Too much worry. I hope you have good news for us.'

'Could be, but not what you except. Can I speak to him?'

Charlie could not conceal his anxiety. No one holding an Irish Hospital Sweepstakes ticket could have panted more eagerly to hear the result.

'What's the form? Any joy from these fiends in Whitehall?'

'I fear not. I have to say this. It would not be realistic to imagine they will change their attitude.'

'I thought as much.' The resignation in his voice suggested that he had known from the outset what the answer would be but had still been determined to go through the motions. It was important for him to be able to place the onus on someone else. 'I don't suppose my beloved brother was much help.'

'I went to see him. And I'm convinced that the U.W.P. attitude to independent producers, including Ben More, is not a personal one. I would ask you to believe that.'

'I didn't think he would be cooperative. But I had a slight hope that after all this time . . .'

'Anyhow,' Quentin interrupted, 'I've got something much more promising for you. Loch Dhuie.'

'I know.'

'I mean the diatomite.'

'That's right. They were here this morning.'

'The devils. Beating the pistol. I mentioned Loch Dhuie casually to Sacher a couple of days ago. I was considering what best to do. Then today I got a summons to attend a meeting with him – and you, if you'll come to Edinburgh – on Friday. I haven't had time to get in touch with you before this. But I'm appalled that they descended on you without warning.'

'Descended is the right word. They arrived by helicopter. Said they were from Sacher Incorporated. That was rather funny, as I had no idea what Sacher was. They thought I was an aborigine. Then they mentioned your name. So I went up with them, and we flew over the Loch. Frightened a large herd of deer in a corrie where I'd never have looked. The two sportsmen were pretty frightened. Not by the helicopter, but by their boss. Moved so fast you'd have thought I'd put a ferret after them. They said everything in their organisation was done by computer, and it wouldn't wait for them, or anyone else.'

'Did you get anything out of them?'

'Nothing positive, except that diatomite is scarce. They took away samples and asked a lot of questions, very sensible most of them, about the climate, access and labour. I filled them up with Old Portree for good measure. Do you think they're serious?'

'Sacher is always serious about anything that can be made to appear as a plus after the dollar symbol. He's just taken over Aphrodite Products, the cosmetic firm.'

'They were astounded that I didn't know all about that. I said we had long ceased to take note of minor tribal skirmishes.'

'Evidently he needs more of your stuff for his talc, and can't readily get it elsewhere. On the other hand, the chances of your finding another purchaser are remote. Now, what about Edinburgh? Can you be there by lunch on Friday? Fiona should come too, as she owns half the Loch. The invitation extends to a film jamboree in the evening. Stay at the Caledonian as his guests.'

'We'll be there.'

'Right. I'll get a memorandum put together so that we all know what we're talking about.'

Before he left the office Quentin made another telephone call.

'Is that McDhuie House Reception?'

'Quentin. Don't be so formal,' Fiona answered. 'What splendid news!'

'You've heard, then?'

'Kirsty's been here.'

'I've an important question to ask you. Are you prepared to ask the distinguished firm of merchant bankers, Albizzi, to act for you in the matter of diatomite? You're not formally our client yet.'

'You know quite well that I'm happy to leave it to you. I don't know how I'll spend all that lovely money. We've got dry rot in the hotel, though how anything remains dry here I can't imagine. We'll put that right for a start. Then I think I'll buy a Range Rover. The van is on the point of expiring – but it has to get us to Inverness in time for the plane tomorrow morning.'

'Doesn't The Keep have something more comfortable?' He remembered his own rattling journey from Kyleakin.

'Not at the moment. As soon as the birdmen left – more of that in a moment – Charlie went off to Portree to see his lawyer, only to find he was away on holiday and the office was closed. He had a few drinks in the bar at the Royal and hit a sheep float on the way back. No real damage done. The aged Bentley's made of iron. But he went off the road and got a puncture, and it seems it's almost impossible to reach the spare wheel. It jams itself under the boot. Anyhow, Kirsty says he had to get the garage-man from Portree to pull out the spare with a winch. He kept staggering about the road cursing the idle lawyer, and

124

meanwhile the midges were driving him mad. It was a shame, because he'd had a grand day till then.'

'How did he fare with the Sacher emissaries?'

'It was hilarious. They landed near the old kennels and Charlie found them fighting their way through the rhododendrons to reach The Keep. When he saw the markings on the helicopter he thought they were deserters from the American Army.'

'They came in an Army chopper?'

'The U.S. Army is always glad to provide transportation for Mr Sacher, Sir. That's what they said. Once they'd established their identity Charlie went up with them, I'm not doing justice to this, but they were a bit worried when he made them keep circling to inspect the line of the river where it comes through the Loch. You can only make it out from the air. Anyhow, he came back to The Keep, burst into the sitting room, and told Kirsty that from the contours he now knew exactly where the fish lay.'

'They must have thought they were on an Indian Reserve.'

'Don't underestimate our Charlie. That was just to prove that diatomite wasn't the only thing in his life. Then he marched them into the office. They kept insisting they were in a hurry, but he gave them a complete rundown on the Estate and all its workings. When Kirsty saw Mrs Macleod taking in a second bottle of Old Portree she thought it was time to rescue them.'

'You mean they shambled off in a haze of malt?'

'They had to be helped on to the helicopter.'

'The cunning old stag. He wasn't nearly so explicit when I spoke to him.'

'As he waved goodbye he said to Kirsty that they would have a better idea of how a Highland enterprise could be run at a profit. Not to be bought for a sheaf of dollars.'

'They would have time to sober up before they reported to Sacher Inc. But it won't impress Sam. He lisps in numbers.'

'The sad thing, and this is what's so worrying, is that after the fiasco at Portree he's had something of a relapse. Kirsty is frightened that he's lost his nerve.'

'Not to worry. We'll do our best. There are complications, but you should be on to a good prospect. You've got to attend the meeting as well – and be at your most sprite-like. And there's an interim bonus already. I'll see you tomorrow.'

Part Three

Chapter XI

Precisely on time, Hermes took off from Heathrow, soaring over the mottled landscape of flooded quarries and sewage farms. The flight to Edinburgh would take an hour and Quentin would have time to sort out his impressions of the highly eclectic company. When Sacher and Houlihan met him at the Airport he had been surprised to find that in addition to Bianca and her mother, Signora Montone, David McLeish was to be a fellow-passenger.

He would have recognised Bianca from her photographs. Simply dressed in a beige trouser suit and a white silk shirt decorated with a single gold brooch, she gave him a wide, impersonal smile that assigned him at once to the category of her incipient admirers. The starring role, her eyes said, was hers, but she was prepared to welcome humble adherents in supporting parts. Signora Montone's presence was understandable. She had come to share the triumph of her daughter's première. Very much *á la mode* in her tailored costume, she still retained an odalisque-like figure. Her hair was layered to match her classical features, and delicate sepia shades completed the ensemble. Together they made a striking pair. Bianca had inherited much from her mother.

The presence on board of David, smartly turned out in the kind of tweed suit worn by captains of industry visiting the provinces, was not so easy to explain. Quentin was not aware of any vestigial business arising from the purchase of Aphro that would require further communing between him and Sacher. No doubt a whisky reason could be adduced to make his journey to Edinburgh coincide with Bianca's, but this would not have prompted a seat in Hermes. Nor would Sacher, who must by now be aware of David's interest in his protegée, have been inclined to ask him of his own volition. If Bianca had suggested that he should travel with them she was either very confident or very naïve.

Quentin's concern was to ascertain whether the implications of the David–Bianca–Sacher triangle could have any bearing on the diatomite discussions. It was possible that if David felt that Bianca was to be his, he might be more benevolently disposed towards his brother, or at least consider the activities of The Keep as being of even less interest than usual. Conversely, should Sacher believe that his liaison was about to be consummated he might take a less decimal, less Zeus-inspired view of other immediate problems. But on present information it was unlikely that the head of Sacher Inc. would let anything interfere with the clicking of the percentage point. The permutations would need careful analysis. He was ready.

Houlihan came from the office, separated by a transparent screen at the rear of the fuselage, to apologise for his Chairman's preoccupation. Mr Sacher hoped his guests would forgive him for a few minutes.

'What', asked Quentin, 'is Our Leader up to now? He hasn't put in a bid for the Airport, has he?'

'Not exactly.' Quentin followed Houlihan's glance over his shoulder at his master crouched over a battery of instruments that could have come from the bridge of a battleship. 'He's operating by satellite. Zeus is helping him take over a hotel chain in Australia. That's an R.F.S. country – Ripe For Sacher. Some local politicians are very anti-American. He's gonna beat the daylights out of them. They think they're tough if they speak Strine, but Sam'll give them a kangaroo kick in the crotch.' Houlihan had an earthy vocabulary.

'Frightening. I suppose he does come to a stop sometimes? To perform his natural functions, for example?'

'Sure.' Houlihan winked. 'If he has to, he can do two things at once. Only one hand to fasten his fly. And he's got your little plan in his skull. Otherwise you wouldn't be here.'

'Mamma!' Bianca's call interrupted them. Her mother was holding a handkerchief to her eye and was obviously in some pain. As the others crowded round, Bianca searched in Signora Montone's handbag to produce an eyedropper, a phial of liquid and a bottle of pills.

'Can I be of any assistance, my dear?' Sacher had appeared, unnoticed.

'Mamma had an operation for glaucoma recently. Any change in air pressure can affect it, but with the drops the discomfort soon goes away. Please don't worry.'

David and Quentin watched concernedly but helplessly as Bianca administered the soothing treatment.

'A glass of water, please.' Signora Montone swallowed a couple of pills and gave a sign that no more need be done. Bianca stood up. Quentin noticed his companion take her gently by the elbow. She pressed his hand against her side. Sacher saw the affectionate gesture. His eyes were riveted on it. He gripped the table behind him so tightly that the knuckles showed white through the skin. It could have been no more than a fraction of a second, but Quentin was suddenly conscious that they were all poised in mid-air.

'I'm distressed', Sacher had some difficulty in clearing his throat, 'that our pressurising system is less than 100 per cent. What do you think, Barney?'

'This goddam plane's certified as 100 per cent.'

'Sam', Bianca linked her arm in his, 'you're not to go tearing everything to bits. It's happened before in other aircraft.' She kissed him lightly on the forehead. 'Mamma, as you can see, is recovering already.'

'In that case,' he had regained his composure, 'perhaps some champagne might help.'

'That, Mr Sacher, is the first sensible thing you've said this morning.'

'Unless David would prefer one of his own brands of whisky?

131

We're ready for all eventualities.'

'You're very thoughtful.' David took no notice of the provocation in Sacher's studied politeness. 'I should be happy with some of the Veuve Clicquot.' For the moment the crossfire had ceased.

'Where are we?' Sacher spoke into the microphone in the side of the lounge while the steward circulated with a tray.

'Just passing Birmingham to starboard, Sir.' The Captain's voice answered.

'Aphro have a factory near here, on the edge of the Motorway.' Sacher peered through the porthole to see if the latest recruits to his family were busy at their workbenches. 'It lost 135 days from strikes last year. David, by what misuse of the English language do you call that industrial action, when it is palpably inaction?'

'I hope the performance of the West Bromwich factory was made clear during our negotiations,' David replied levelly.

'It was indeed. I'm sorry if I sounded too critical.' He had mastered his irritation as he refilled their glasses. 'I'm sure that's not a problem peculiar to Aphro. But we're going to put it right. You won't remember Charles Bedaux, the original time and motion man. Before the last war he had some original ideas about improving output, but his public relations were poor. There were riots if the workers knew his men were on the premises. We do the job better. When the work force see Zeus's figures and realise their own paypackets are at risk, it has a wonderful effect on the shop floor. You see, even Zeus is human sometimes.' So, thought Quentin, was Sam Sacher, who now returned apologetically to his control chamber.

Sitting beside David, Quentin asked him how he came to be a passenger on Hermes.

'Whisky affairs, I imagine?'

'Strictly speaking, yes. I've arranged some meetings in connection with a Trust we may establish. Bianca said I must come to the party after her première, and an invitation to climb aboard followed.' If David saw anything unusual in this sequence of events, there was no sign of it. 'You might be

132

interested in the Trust.' He warmed to his subject as he described the general ambience he had in mind.

'But this is absolutely fascinating!' Quentin took up the theme with some enthusiasm. 'As you know, in another world, before I joined Albizzi, I was intrigued by the whole question of patronage in the Renaissance. How far is the patron inspired by the exercise of power to inflate his own ego, and how far does he genuinely want to encourage original talent?'

'I've already warned you about your sceptical sensibility,' David laughed.

'I wasn't being offensive, just curious. But why does your plan have a Scottish accent? Nostalgic nationalism would scarcely be in character.'

'It will be called the Barleycorn Trust, relating it to the whisky that provides the funds, and I thought there should be a demonstrable Scottish link. Artists who get grants from the Trust need not be Scottish, but their entries will, I hope, be vetted by the Scottish Academy.'

'I know you're a collector in your own right. I have one painting by the Scottish artist, James Pryde. He's had something of a revival recently. He painted small, shrunken figures against a background larger than life. Apparently that was a perspective induced by the bottle. But I like his dark, cavernous interiors. They remind me of The Keep, if you'll forgive the comparison.'

'Really? I hadn't noticed.' David remained impassive. Quentin had meant his ingenuous remark to give rise to some discussion about life at Lower Borve, but he realised he was still an apprentice salmon fisher. The fly had been too heavily dressed.

'I want to talk to David.' Bianca stood beside them. 'I'm sure Mr Houlihan will let you see the Captain's cabin, if you ask him.'

Quentin took the hint. Barney escorted him for'ard and he listened with bewilderment to the explanation of how the principal controls worked. They were starting to lose height as they neared their destination. The Firth of Forth gleamed below them. Barney shuddered.

'I don't know about you, but sure as hell I hate flying over the drink. I'm not a good swimmer and I don't want to be buried at sea.'

'They sew you up in a sail cloth,' Quentin replied, 'and put the last stitch through your nose.'

'In mortuaries they tie the identity tag round your big toe – or your dick. I know. We own a chain of mortician's parlours. Stiffs are very profitable in the States.'

'A macabre business.'

'You're sure right it is. Sam and the film star, I mean.' He nodded towards the main compartment.

'You don't approve?'

'Can I be frank with you? I want you and your friends to keep Sam busy all day. I'll be right in there with you. What keeps Sam off the glamour girl is good news with Sacher Inc.'

'You mean that Zeus doesn't recognise comets?'

'You put it better than I can.'

Sam came tripping down the passage to meet them as they rejoined the main party. An unlikely sight, but tripping was the only word to describe his excitement.

'They've given in, Barney. Our next expedition will be to Sydney to incorporate their leading hotel group. God bless trade union solidarity.' He rubbed his hands together in undisguised glee.

'Is there a point about union intervention that escapes me?' David sounded mildly supercilious.

'A signal reached the Australian union – the one that represents the hotel industry. It said just how many jobs would be lost if my bid was blocked. It was sent, in the name of international brotherhood, by a powerful union in the States which is a good friend of ours. I have always', he gave a mischievous grin and pricked his ears, 'endorsed the corporate entity of the unions. They can be played off against each other, like all vested interests.'

'I assume this is the multi-national philosophy. Isn't such omnipotence alarming?' A sarcastic undertone was discernible in David's question.

'On the contrary. It's a challenge. As stimulating as Veuve

134

Clicquot. Aren't you interested in exercising power?'

'Only so far as is necessary to obtain one's objectives. Not for its own sake.'

That, thought Quentin, was probably a true assessment of David's approach. His appetite for power was limited, and strangely conventional. He wanted to be Chairman of U.W.P. He would be. If there was no more to it than that, he should not, in theory, find it necessary to demand a further tribute from his brother. The flight had served a useful purpose.

Hermes came to rest on the runway. Bianca was composing herself for her public appearance.

'I did tell you, Sam, that there would be a reception committee. Will you come with me? After all, the film's half yours. David, will you look after Mamma?'

The gangway was wheeled out. The door opened to the loud skirl of the bagpipes. Photographers swarmed round, clicking their cameras like cicadas, but it was the pipes and drums drawn up on the tarmac that caught the ear and eye. Bianca paused at the top of the steps to wave and give the photographers their chance. There was a ripple of applause from the spectators on the roof terrace. She descended slowly, but with easy grace, to be greeted by the Airport Commandant.

'This is too much,' murmured David from the door of the plane. A very small boy, so small that he had at first been overlooked, stepped forward to bow and present a bouquet of white heather. Bianca bent down to accept it. On a sudden impulse she lifted him and kissed on the cheek.

'I know she's photogenic,' David muttered, 'but the Virgin Mary and Child is going too far.'

'I'm waiting for Zeus to change water into wine.' Quentin was surprised that Zeus had not already been given the relevant data.

The Commandant led Bianca towards the gigantic figure of the Drum Major in his full Highland dress and black bearskin. He raised his baton and the piping came to an end. The Drum Major saluted.

135

'Welcome to Scotland, Miss.' His rich vernacular was unmistakeable.

'Thank you very much. What were you playing?'

'"My Highland Home". It's a tune greatly beloved by Her Majesty, The Queen, Miss.'

'Would you please say how much I appreciated it? Something I will never forget.' She shook his hand. 'I do admire your wonderful uniform.' As if by an afterthought, though Quentin now suspected that few of her actions were as innocent as they appeared, she gave his sporran a tug with both hands. The cameras snapped in unison. He saluted again, with even more fervour.

A cortège of black limousines was waiting. As they boarded, Quentin enquired whether this was the normal form of reception. The Commandant said that during the Festival all incoming flights were met by a piper. The full strength of the Edinburgh Pipe Band had been ordered, and paid for, by the film company. But there would be a dividend. The front pages of the national press would feature the star and the sporran. Another reason for Sacher's interest in Bianca suggested itself. It had been a regal performance. She would be a worthy consort.

Chapter XII

'The Edinburgh Festival, is it for the benefit of the artists or the audience?' On the way from the airport Signora Montone shared the second car with David and Quentin.

'A good question,' David replied. I don't really know the answer. I do know it's not all sweetness and light behind the scenes. There's always a squabble about the programme. The City Fathers, who meet part of the cost, think they should have a say. They want to include *The Desert Song* or *Rose Marie on Ice*. The Festival Society, who are nominally in charge, hanker after something more ambitious – Schoenberg or Stockhausen, so they compromise with unrelieved Brahms. I speak objectively, because I'm tone-deaf.'

'Completely? That must be sad.' Quentin perceived in this unexpected confession a possible reason for David's slightly repellent air of self-reliance. To be tone-deaf could have an isolating effect. One method of communication was closed to him. Possibly others were too. That could account for the way he had underestimated Sacher at the European Board meeting.

'Who started this great Scottish Saturnalia?'

'Lost in the sands of time. There are many who claim, or infer, it was their idea, but you can discount most of them. An unlikely trio conceived it – a far-sighted Lord Provost, Lady Rosebery the wife of the racehorse owner, and the Hungarian impresario Rudolf Bing. It's survived all kinds of crises, divas departing in a huff, artists withdrawing their paintings, all the fun of the fair. I'm unashamedly pro-Festival, but it could do with some sharper organisation.'

'A job for the Barleycorn Trust, suitably enlarged?'

'Great Scot! I've no ambitions in that direction.'

137

'Or Sacher could always feed the Festival data to Zeus and see what harmony emerges.'

'If you put that idea into his head he might take you seriously.'

'In Italy', Signora Montone had not spoken for some time, 'we have a proverb about what happens when a bullfrog becomes too greedy. I won't repeat it. As you can imagine, it isn't very polite. But you can guess what it says.'

Loganair's scheduled flight from Inverness to Turnhouse brought Kirsty, Charlie and Fiona, each with their own preoccupations.

After the upheaval caused by the helicopter fluttering over The Keep had subsided, they were left in a state of confusion. It seemed scarcely credible that Loch Dhuie – a remote hill loch where the stillness was disturbed only by the trout rising – should suddenly become a marketable asset. The unfortunate experience of the earlier prospectors, who could not extract the white powder at a profit, made it more difficult to translate the small blob on the Ordnance Survey map into potential yield figures. The calculations would have to be left to Quentin, and it remained to be seen whether Mr Sacher, whose name was known only from articles in *Vogue* wanted to do business. Meanwhile, they had other, more personal anxieties.

Kirsty was worried lest the excitement of the journey would have a bad effect on Charlie. The doctor had said that he had suffered a mild heart attack. He would have more, and one of them could be fatal. For the time being, any emotional disturbance must be avoided. Kirsty had played her part by avoiding any reference to the Morag incident. She tried not to think of the night when she drove the girl to the hospital at Portree, and heard her anguished cry. It had sounded like 'Charlie'. Unable to nurse her thoughts by herself, she had said to Fiona – without warning – that she sometimes wondered if Charlie was attracted by Morag. She was an unusually pretty little thing, she was young, and she had a roving eye. Fiona's reaction was too innocent, her denial too positive.

138

It confirmed Kirsty's suspicions. She must put these disloyal thoughts behind her. Charlie, as had often happened before, would need her support. Whatever form it took, she would be prepared.

Charlie had begun to think that there were no more clouds of glory to be trailed. He found it difficult to throw off fits of depression, and he was conscious that Old Portree was too prominent in his diet. A sense of failure was creeping over him. Despite his years of careful planning, his one major attempt to achieve financial security, the Distillery expansion, had been stillborn. More painfully, despite Quentin's disclaimer, he felt his brother had been in part responsible. There had been no sign that David recognised the continuous effort that had gone into his guardianship of the inheritance, no friendly gesture. His brother ignored him. Why should he court further humiliation if, as might happen, David had to be consulted about an agreement with Sacher to work the minerals? Charlie had spent much of the eight hours since they left The Keep trying to make up his mind whether it was worth one more throw.

He was also worried that his wife had seemed different since Morag's miscarriage. Not that she had said anything to suggest that she believed he had been the father, but if Kirsty did not have second sight her powers of perception might have led her to guess the truth. Looking through the porthole, he thought of Morag. It had happened only a few times, seven or eight at most, and it was the first coming together he remembered best. He had stopped at the Distillery office to go over his notes for the Farmers Union dinner. He had nearly finished when Morag came in. She understood he wanted the insurance file. This was untrue: he had made no such request. Then it happened quickly. She brushed against his arm as she leaned over his shoulder. He realised he had always lusted after her. Involuntarily he pulled her down and kissed her. She put her arms round his neck and her tongue darted in his mouth. Mr McKellar was in Inverness, she murmured, there was no one else in the office, but shouldn't he lock the door? He stumbled across to turn the key. In a moment of caution he drew the curtains, though the window was not overlooked.

He thought of her young, attractive body which he had enjoyed. The whole affair had been sordid and undignified – their assignations had been furtive, snatched moments in the Distillery Office when McKellar was in Inverness, yet he did not regret his momentary self-indulgence. For a short time, Morag had made him feel young again, young and desirable, and their times together were imprinted vividly on his memory. But he could not excuse himself for wounding Kirsty, for creating the doubts which must now be in her mind.

Then McKellar said she was becoming impossible at her office work and would have to go. Charlie dared not dissent. She had protested at first, but she knew there was an ending. She cut short his tentative offer of help. He shouldn't imagine he was her only admirer. Now his mouth was dry at the recollection.

Fiona's mood was more pleasurable and far removed from any expectations she might have as a joint diatomite heiress. She was reliving the last day on the hill with Angus. She had shot her stag at Callum's Point, and they were strapping the carcass on the pony when the ghillie looked over the saddle at her.

'It's a pity Mr Lawrence isn't here to have a second chance at a deer. Will he be coming back?'

'Yes, Angus. I'm sure of it.'

'That's what I'm thinking myself.' He gave the belt a final tug and they started for home.

As she thought about it, she was not so certain. She could not make up her mind what they had in common, what it was in him that quickened her pulse. A scholar, a banker, used to a much suaver milieu than Borve, in his days at The Keep he had quickly made himself at home. During their last dinner they had developed an intimacy she had not known before. But he would continue to live in the South. Would she be willing to exchange McDhuie House for London W.14? More important, could they forge the kind of partnership she wanted, or would

she have to surrender herself – a contingency she had always
fought against? Steady, Fiona. That way madness lay. She
blushed to find herself wondering if she would have time to have
her hair done.

'Mr Sacher's compliments, Sir. Could I have your baggage
checks, please?' The chauffeur led Charlie and his party
through the Airport building.

'Look here!' A familiar voice brought them to a halt. 'What is
all this luggage marked 'Barcelona' doing on the conveyor?'
General Carnoustie was addressing a flustered attendant.

'I don't know, Sir.'

'Is it going to Barcelona, or has it come from Spain?'

'I couldn't say, Sir.'

'But don't you care? You'll correct me if I'm wrong, but the
London flight has just arrived – after an intolerable delay, it's
true – here in Edinburgh. Is that right?'

'Yes, Sir.'

'Good. There are two things to consider. The absence of luggage from London, and the presence of the Barcelona baggage.
You wouldn't think there's some sinister connection between
these, would you?'

'I . . .'

'You couldn't say. Quite so. Then perhaps you would
explain what I'm to do in Edinburgh, naked, without a suitcase?'

'Excuse me, Sir. The London labels are coming through the
delivery hatch now. I hope you'll find yours there.'

'I hope so too. But dammit, what about these poor Span-
iards? There may be a great gang of them circling round
Europe looking for their *muletas* and *mantillas*. And another
thing. Look at that notice, 'Golf clubs will be carried'. How
dare you put up a notice like that? I haven't come to play golf.
Why should you cater only for golfers, or make it compulsory to
carry golf clubs?'

'General Havvy! That's quite enough!' Fiona took him by
the arm. 'Stop behaving like the Duke of Cumberland. What

141

are you doing here?'

'Good God, Fiona! And Kirsty and Charlie. How splendid to see some sane faces in this asylum. What am I doing? Subject to these cretins, I'm taking the Salute at the Tattoo tonight. That's if I can find my kit.'

Carnoustie's military madness never lasted for long. His luggage was found. He was staying at the same hotel, and accepted the offer of a lift in the Sacher car. He enquired why the Skye contingent had come to Edinburgh. He had a last barb as they reached the West End of Princes Street.

'And you're going to see the stylish Mr Lawrence again, Fiona. Is that right?'

Fiona found Quentin, looking very elegant in a grey flannel suit and a foulard tie, waiting with Houlihan in the hotel foyer. She wondered what he would say if she pushed back the curl of black hair that flopped over his forehead.

'Quentin, look what I've found.' she dragged Carnoustie forward.

'Very nice to see you again, Sir.' Quentin remembered that the General was a great deal shrewder than he pretended.

'And you too, my boy. Kind of your friend to provide transport for an old *shikari*. I'm lucky to be here. The Admiral who should have been on duty at the Tattoo tonight has called off, so they dragged me up from the Reserve List.'

'Won't you join us for dinner tonight, Sir?' Houlihan asked.

'Rations all right here, are they? No. Thank you very much, but I've got to dine with the G.O.C. I used to know his father. When the Generals begin to look young, it's time to move on. Forward to the Grassy Plot.' He made for the lift, a frightened bearer following with his luggage.

Houlihan said they were all to regard themselves as Mr Sacher's guests during their stay. The diatomite meeting would be at three o'clock. Mr Sacher would like them to dine with him in the hotel and attend the *Poppaea* reception afterwards.

'And what', asked Quentin, 'is Our Leader doing meanwhile?'

'If you were to say he was studying computer projections you would have a 99 per cent chance of being right. But right now he's putting it to some Dingo Minister. They want the news about the hotel takeover to break in Australia. Sam figures New York is right.'

'That has some earth-shaking significance?'

'When you can shake the earth, like Sam, it is only the crap that worries you. So? You guessed it. New York gets the statement two hours on.'

'And the Senator from the Outback?'

'If he calls again he gets the answering service. See you.'

'Is he always as brisk as that?' Kirsty watched the retreating figure.

'Houlihan's a droll character.' Quentin laughed at Kirsty's puzzled expression. 'But compared to the boss man, he's as gentle as a lamb. The point for you to note is that he's on your side – with one important proviso. He wants Sacher and the film star kept as far apart as possible. So it's up to you and Fiona to entice him away from his charmer. But you'll find the competition pretty fierce. Now, here's the paper with all the pluses and minuses. I suggest you get your heads down and read it.'

'One other thing, Quentin.' Charlie had been silent so far. 'My damned lawyer in Portree has taken himself off to the flesh-pots on the Costa Brava. I've arranged to consult a legal fellow here to see if we can get some wisdom on the Will. Would you come with me?'

Alexander Galloway, Senior Partner in Galloway, Shaw, and Porteous, Writers to the Signet, was ill at ease. He knew the reason lay in his own shortcomings and that made it worse. He had not actually given anyone legal advice for many years. He cultivated a mollifying, deferential air to pacify the firm's most important clients, leaving the business of construing the law to assistants, but when Charlie McLeish telephoned from Skye he had to say he would see him. Charlie was married to the daughter of a former senior partner. Galloway sighed as he looked through his window at the neat parterre in the middle of Charlotte Square. It was too bad that he sould have to answer queries in person, Particularly when he had only the vaguest idea of the subject for discussion. He heard the abominable Binns clock at the West End chiming the hour. With any luck their plane would be late and he could slip away to join his cronies in the New Club.

Loganair did nothing to relieve Mr Galloway's distemper. Charlie was punctual in keeping his appointment. When he introduced Quentin as a partner in Albizzi Bros., the Scottish lawyer regretted even more that he had agreed to the consultation. It was quite possible that Albizzi had already taken advice and would be the more ready to detect any flaws in his judgment.

'The matter you mentioned, Charlie, if I have correctly understood it, raises difficulties of some complexity – as regards both ownership and the nature of the relevant testamentary provision.'

'I thought it was simply a question of saying whether my brother's consent is required to granting a mineral lease. I know he has to agree before a sale can take place, and I wanted to know whether the same restriction applies to granting permission, even on a lease basis, for the extraction of minerals.'

'Things are seldom what they seem. As a layman, if you will forgive me, you would naturally simplify. My job is not to complicate the issue, but to see that all the possible hazards are examined. Let's address ourselves to the question of ownership. Who, for example, holds the valid title to the Loch?'

'I've always assumed that half belongs to the McDhuie Estate and half to us. Certainly I have always been told that the march runs through the middle. Fiona and I are perfectly content to proceed on a fifty-fifty basis.'

'But who is the feudal superior?' Galloway asked reprovingly. 'That is the first question. Do either of you pay feu duty to the other?'

'I can't be certain, but I do believe we get a feu payment from the McDhuie Estate. I've never enquired what it represents. Only a very small sum.'

'Very possibly. But that would need to be clarified, and we should also check whether there are any servitudes on the land. We can do that by having a search made in the Register of Sasines, but it will take a little time. Then there's the Will. You haven't a copy with you, I suppose?'

'No. It's in Portree. I thought you could advise straightaway on the simple – I still regard it as simple – issue,' Charlie said irritably.

'Even if we had the pertinent clauses before us I would be bound to urge you to seek Counsel's opinion. We can, if you like, put in hand the preparation of a memorandum posing the exact questions on which advice is sought, but I know that James McSherry, who's the leader in this field, is snowed under with work.' He spread his hands to semaphore his inability to produce either Counsel or an opinion on demand.

'Mr Galloway,' Quentin intervened sharply, 'Are you aware that there is some urgency about this? We have to meet the other principal this afternoon.'

'The worst thing a lawyer can do, Mr Lawrence, is to make a hurried pronouncement. I'm sure you appreciate that. An ill-considered view can be extremely detrimental to the client's interests, and you wouldn't want me to improvise in such a dangerous fashion.'

'In that case, Charlie, I don't see how we can carry this discussion further at the moment. If, following this afternoon's meeting we need further advice, you may wish to ask Mr Galloway to give the matter his prompt attention once again.' Quentin could not forbear a last attempt to puncture the lawyer's complacency. He was still smarting when the elegant Georgian door closed behind them.

'I wouldn't call him a ball of fire, your learned friend.'

'You're dead right. Kirsty's father said he was a jumped-up conveyancing clerk who swam about in a glycerine bath. But what do we do now?'

'Play it by ear. Always the best way when the score isn't complete. Incidentally, you're not tone-deaf are you?'

'No, Why?'

'An exercise in sensitivity.'

Mr Galloway was pleased that he would still be in time for a glass of sherry before lunch. If Charlie really believed a huge American Corporation wanted to speculate in peat-bogs, he was suffering from advanced mental atrophy. Galloway, Shaw and Porteous would not be troubled with it again. He had more useful things to contemplate. He hoped the friend at the New Club would have news that he had been elected to the Board of the Investment Trust whose Chairman he had served so reverently for years. Levering himself out of his armchair, he thought it was a pity that the Board no longer collected their fees in the form of a pile of sovereigns, but membership would finally endorse his elevation to the Edinburgh Establishment. He broke wind in proleptic satisfaction.

Chapter XIII

Charlie brightened up at Quentin's suggestion that they should lunch at the Lorraine, a restaurant in Castle Street highly recommended by Claude Albizzi.

'Good idea,' he agreed. 'Haven't been there for years. Used to be known as the Abattoir during the war. Great place for recruiting ladies of the town.' His dewlaps wobbled at the memory of past exploits as a swordsman. 'But they've changed all that. Very respectable, although they've still got some of the staff.'

The Head Waiter was one who had not changed. The foyer and the bar were full of Festival buffs, but he came forward at once.

'A great pleasure, Major McLeish. There's always a table for old friends, if you don't mind the front room. We're pretty full', he added in an undertone, 'with freaks and foreigners.'

'Very good of you, Donald. How are you keeping?'

'Mustn't complain. A touch of the rheumatics now and then. Not like old times.'

'Remarkable fellow,' Charlie mused over his large pink gin. 'I once saw him throw out three Naval Officers single-handed. All very much in their cups, of course. Two of them were holding up a small midshipman to pee into the hand-drier in the Gents. They switched on the hot air fan to make the spray blow back on the snottie. Seemed funny at the time.'

Charlie's genial mood lasted throughout lunch. He was

going to stay in Edinburgh for a few days. Kirsty and Fiona could sample the Festival and he would take up a long-standing invitation to shoot grouse on the Lammermuirs.

'One of the snags about Skye is that we've no grouse to speak of. My father was always indignant that there was not enough heather, and when the young birds hatched there was too much rain. He used to speak enviously of the days when Lovat, Lochiel and The Mackintosh – all dead now – competed in their butts. He was sometimes asked as an extra gun. But his real heroes were two English peers. Lord Walsingham was the first. He shot a thousand and seventy grouse in one day. That was a record and I can still remember the total. Even that didn't match the Marquess of Ripon. He was credited with over half a million birds in the course of his lifetime. He had a good death too – collapsed on the moor after shooting his fifty-second bird of the morning.'

'Do you really enjoy such mass destruction?'

'I've never done anything on that scale. Much prefer walking up with a dog. It's the sport that counts. Testing your eye and reflexes. That's what my beloved brother could never understand.'

'Was that what caused the trouble between him and your father?'

'Not entirely. The old man couldn't stand humbug – and that included loafing in the Library at The Keep when the fish were taking. Then David defied him and was never forgiven. It was a trivial occasion. The County Council started evening classes – they'd be called Further Education now – and my father made them include fly-tying in the syllabus. He wanted us both to go and show an example. David refused and there was an unholy row. All the Jacobite precedents were quoted to support parental discipline. David observed that Prince Charlie couldn't tie his own shoelaces, far less a salmon fly. He was locked up in his room for days. Mother made it worse by offering to go in his place and she was berated for mollycoddling.'

'The McLeishes do take their field sports very seriously.'

'I'm not ashamed of that. It's been a great thing in my life. If you're born to it you have to carry on.' Quentin noticed the vein throbbing in his forehead as his voice became more defiant. 'You must realise my father was a very big man – everything had to be made for him except his ties and handkerchiefs – and he took himself very seriously. He had no sense of humour. He once told a guest that he was a great admirer of Sir Arthur Sullivan. The wretched man, not unnaturally, thought he was referring to the D'Oyly Carte operas and made some jokes about *The Mikado*, but my father was quite ignorant of Gilbert and Sullivan. He meant that he had read that Sullivan, who, after seeing a peeress killed by a runaway horse, had invented and patented a Safety Shaft to release the animal from the vehicle in an emergency. No household should be without one, he said.'

'You make him sound very formidable.'

'What finally turned the old man against David was a time when the laugh was on him. He used to carry out all his duties to the letter. When he was Chairman of the District Council he appointed a rather dubious fellow to be District Clerk. The locals didn't like it and the parish minister came with a deputation to protest. But the old man wouldn't budge. Then the minister, as a last resort, asked if he realised that the offending Clerk was a notorious sodomite. My father was not impressed. "I'm surprised at you, a minister of the Church" he replied. "There's one thing I've always believed in. Religious tolerance. Catholic, Protestant, Rechabite, Sodomite – it makes no difference to me." The deputation withdrew in bad order.'

'That is worth a glass of brandy with your coffee!' Quentin had not seen him so vivacious.

'Not finished yet. When David heard what had happened, he couldn't believe it. He asked if his father, after a lifetime in the Army, didn't realise that sod was short for sodomite. Then he laughed so much that he was banished from the table. But he kept finding ways to bring the word into the conversation. If he saw anyone with a spade he'd say "Ah! Turning the sods, no doubt." Very funny to begin with, but he overdid it.'

'I begin to see what was in mind when the Will was drawn

up.'

'I wonder if David was really surprised. As time went on, he kept more and more to himself. He did well at school and at University, and I think my father began to be afraid of him. When the news came through that he had got a First at Cambridge, the old man turned away without speaking. To be fair, he was probably frightened by the uncertainty of anything that originated in the mind and couldn't be related to the game larder. That and the impersonal way David produced his arguments. If he'd had a touch of dash – just one – my father might have made allowances. Then he wouldn't go to David's graduation. I suppose that's why David refused to come to my passing-out parade at the Shop.'

'Even the best-ordered families have their misunderstandings.'

Quentin was touched by the wistful note that had crept into Charlie's voice. 'You know, I think there's more to the parallel with the Master of Ballantrae – which our film star is going to appear in – than you might want to admit.'

'Hardly. I read it as a boy. If I've got it right, Stevenson's brothers both come to a bad end in the swamps of New England. The elder one, the Master, is buried alive and the younger is struck down at the graveside. But the real villain in that story is the father. To save his own miserable neck, old Durrisdeer sent one son to fight with the Jacobites and kept the other at home to prove he was a loyal Hanoverian. The Fourteenth McLeish would never have trimmmed like that, so your analogy breaks down. As for David, he may seem callous, and often acts like it, but the Master of Ballantrae had the devil in him, and I wouldn't like to say that of my brother.'

'Talking of the devil, don't look behind you. David's here.' Quentin had seen him emerging from the rear room of the restaurant. 'Not a word about diatomite. Let him be the one to recognise you.' This was not the time to set them at each other.Quentin was not going to let his client go into action unprepared if he could help it.

David could not ignore them. Motioning his companion to go

150

ahead, he stopped at their table.

'Greetings, Charlie. Come to enjoy the delights of the Festival? A belated conversion, surely.'

'I'm shooting at Mossdoun tomorrow.'

'Oh yes.' The intonation might have been polite, or sarcastic. It was too icy to say. 'Well, may all good fortune attend you.' A twitch of his head and he left them.

'The bugger. First time in years, and he didn't ask for Kirsty or the boys.' Charlie's good humour was crushed. 'I wouldn't have him as a pheasant-plucker.' The coffee spoon in his fingers was almost bent double.

'Steady. Put all that out of your mind. We're going to see Sacher this afternoon. That's far more important for your family – and Fiona. We'll go back to the Caledonian and take it from there.'

For the moment he felt that the McLeishes were being far too prickly, grating their nerves at the first, casual opportunity. It confirmed all he had been told. A pox on both their houses. But his sympathy lay with Charlie. He recalled how Stevenson had described the younger brother's attitude to his reverses. Something like a maimed soldier, looking vainly for discharge, lingering derided in the line of battle. It was depressingly apt.

Kirsty and Fiona had a more frugal lunch in the hotel Buttery. It was not the menu that engrossed them.

'You mean you're seriously thinking you might marry him?' Kirsty was not sure whether this was one of Fiona's wilder fantasies. It did not sound like it.

'I didn't realise how seriously until Lachlan started to tease me. Sister Fiona – he only calls me that when he thinks it's his place to give me a wigging – sister Fiona, he said, I see a cloud no bigger than a man's hand, but it's growing to resemble Quentin Lawrence. He'd counted the times I'd asked him about life as a merchant banker. Then he added scornfully that a man who couldn't take a deer from the hill was not for me.'

'That's unfair. Lachlan 's often come home without getting

151

near enough to have a shot. You're not going to select a husband for his skill as a stalker. But you might be thinking of Quentin just now because for the time being he's rather important to us.'

'It's more than that. I would be dishonest not to admit it. During the flight this morning I kept comparing him with the other men in my life. He's far more mature than anyone I've met at St Andrews, and he outshines the escorts who swarm up for the Skye Ball – though that's not difficult.'

'I like him. He's kind, and he's good with Charlie.'

'But he's naturally sarcastic. He has to try hard not to be. I don't know if I could put up with that.'

'My dear, you're not given to introspection like this.' Kirsty had never seen such a grave expression on her face. 'But that's not what matters. Would you follow him anywhere?'

'He's very much an Englishman. I know it's absolutely absurd to say that, as though it were some kind of bar. But if I married him it would mean leaving the Island. We'd only come back on holiday.'

'You always said you and Lachlan wouldn't keep the Hotel going much longer.'

'That was before we heard we might be able to sell Loch Dhuie. If we do, it could be very different. We'd have enough capital and we could stay if we wanted to. I don't know, Kirsty. I get so involved in all the things we do – both at McDhuie House and at The Keep. How do you feel about it?'

'I'm involved. No doubt about that.'

'And you're not a native. Do you regret spending all your married life in The Keep?'

'I don't think much about it, perhaps because it's a long time since I had to make a choice. I knew that Charlie needed me, and that was what mattered. I have no regrets. No one can change what has happened, but I might have been just as content if things had turned out differently and I'd lived elsewhere. I had no ambition to be the mistress of a vast Estate, and I never thought it would be so overpowering. If I were you and had to choose – it's a painful business and I do feel for you – I wouldn't be too distressed if I had to leave Skye. Provided I knew why I was leaving.'

'Dear Kirsty, I'll come and weep on your shoulder if he asks me. Or if he doesn't.'

Chapter XIV

Zeus had been switched off. Or so it seemed as Sacher made it clear to Charlie and Fiona that he saw diatomite not as a speculation, but as a sound investment. He came straight to the crux. Diatomite was a raw material he needed; they were willing to sell; Sacher Inc. could undertake extraction on a scale that would be viable; they only had to find terms that would be acceptable to both sides.

'By that I mean terms', he added with a disarming aside, 'that will allow us all to go away and believe we have got the better of the bargain.'

Other difficulties might appear, but Quentin realised that Charlie and Fiona could have little idea how quickly Sacher had immersed himself in the details, and how he had taken care to put his visitors at their ease. Not having seen Sacher at full throttle, they could not appreciate that they were either being treated with unusual consideration, or being given a soft sell.

'The important factors are all set out in the memorandum,' Sacher went on. 'It may strike you as oddly as it does me that Quentin, who prepared it, should be advising both of us. More than that, he has told me he has been a guest in your house, and I'm glad to have the privilege of entertaining him today. But it doesn't affect his impartial assessment. That's a rare mark of quality.'

Fiona made a face at the object of Sacher's eulogy. Quentin shook his head to deprecate both the laudatory terms and her comment.

'I could go further. It's a testimony to the excellence of your merchant banking firms. I can't say the same of your clearing banks, which', his heavy frown doubtless recalled some unsatisfactory experience in the past, 'believe that credit should be granted with the same frequency as the Last Sacrament. Shall we look at the memo itself? Have you had time to study it, Mr McLeish?'

'I have, and I think I understand it, so far as it goes.'

'It's all there – Sacher Inc.'s estimated capital expenditure in installing plant, labour costs, transport costs. Everything till you reach our factory. The memo rightly stops there,' a grimmer look flitted across his face, 'because what happens thereafter is my concern. On page three you will find the price we have paid in the past, and are now paying, for diatomite. Paragraph seven eliminates historic costs and temporary variations. These figures are supplied by us so that you can assess our offer in its proper context. My proposition Mr McLeish,' as Sacher looked up Quentin thought it would take a courageous man to reject the offer that was coming, whatever it was, 'my proposition is that we should pay you £250,000 for the site where we erect our plant, for the right to extract from your Loch, and for unrestricted access to the approach road. We would also pay a royalty of 85 per cent of what we pay elsewhere for crude diatomite. This protects you from losing, as you would, if there was a sudden escalation in prices in other markets and you were tied to a fixed figure. For my part, the deduction of 15 per cent reflects the cost of doing our own extraction and the long haul to our factory in the south.'

Sacher sat back, clasping his hands together. The dark-blue suit and cream-coloured shirt emphasised his sallow complexion. He looked like a reptile temporarily at ease. Quentin perceived that he was enjoying himself. He was dealing with individuals who would not normally cross his path, not with computer symbols. Unless something upset him, they might be home.

The hum of passing traffic seemed more insistent. Seated

155

round the table, Sacher's audience might have been listening to the cars in Lothian Road accelerating away from the traffic lights. No one spoke. Charlie and Fiona, eyes on the papers before them, were stunned by the size of the offer and the compelling way in which the elements had been identified for them. Seeing that neither was keen to make the first observation, Sacher turned to Fiona.

'Perhaps it would be courteous to ask for your views first, Miss McDhuie.'

'The sums seem fair.' Her shrill tone betrayed her nervousness. 'If Quentin thinks the deal is reasonable, I would be content. But there is one thing I'm worried about. The level of the Loch. You haven't been to Borve, Mr Sacher.'

'Alas, no.' His smile gave her confidence. Her voice became more resonant.

'The lochans on our Estate, and eventually the Borve river itself, are fed from Loch Dhuie. If the Loch level falls it will alter the height of the water downstream. Has anyone any idea what will be the effect of extraction on your scale?' She gazed appealingly at Sam. In her blue and white shirtwaister she looked cooler than she must have felt.

'If I could take that up,' Houlihan answered, 'we're not out to bust your fishings, Miss McDhuie. I like hunting, myself. If the Loch falls we bulldoze another channel.' He mimed the action with his huge hands. 'Then your fishes can have a grand parade right down to the ocean. Simple as that. Just a detail. It won't holds us up.' He was keeping his promise to oil the wheels.

'Would that be acceptable to you?' Sacher asked. 'It's not a point that had occurred to me – the comparative economics of diatomite extraction and freshwater fishing. Do your fishings have any commerical value?'

'It's not what we charge for a rod, or the actual catch that worries me. Fishing is what we do, and I wouldn't want to stay at Borve if I couldn't spend a day on the river or the loch when I wanted to. Mr Sacher, I haven't suggested that there's a compensation factor to be taken into account. But I'll bet the natives of Mogadishu and Mombasa struck a hard bargain for the ambergis which stranded whales spewed up on the beaches, and which early merchants desperately wanted for their perfume.'

'My compliments on your knowledge of our industry. Can I ask where you found this unusual piece of information?'

'In the Library of The Keep yesterday.' She laughed self-consciously, looking around for support. But she didn't need it. Sacher clapped his hands together. Chameleon-like, his expression turned to one of unrelieved benevolence.

'Admirable, Miss McDhuie. You persuade me. All necessary work will be done to preserve your fishings. Now, Mr McLeish?'

Charlie was not at his best. He was still deflated by the encounter with his brother. He was too big for the antique chair. He looked uncomfortable. His checked jacket hung loosely on his dispirited shoulders. His voice was slurred, and his delivery slow.

'Agree with what Fiona says about the figures. All right with me if Quentin says so. But I have to think about the future. How long before the deposits are exhausted?'

'From our reports,' Houlihan replied, 'there is enough for at least thirty years. It could be more.'

'Have to look ahead to my heirs and successors.' Suddenly his voice cleared. 'Would you see any objection to offering the Loch back to our two Estates, at a valuer's price, when you have no further use for it?'

'None at all,' Sacher's bland air was undisturbed. 'We could in terms require you to buy it back when there is no diatomite left – what might be called an 'exhausting lease'. But we won't do that. Your proposal is quit sensible. Our discretion to relinquish the site: yours to reacquire it.'

'Mr Sacher,' Fiona burst in excitedly, 'What will you call the talc you make from our diatomite?'

'It won't have a name. It will be used to maintain supplies of existing makes.'

'Why not a new line altogether? 'Skye Mist'? All the magic of the Herbrides. Neatly wrapped in McDhuie or McLeish

157

tartan.'

'Fiona has difficulty in keeping her imagination under control,' Charlie said apologetically.

'My dear, I like imagination. I respect initiative. You have both. When you come to New York I will show you my computer in operation. You will see how many factors have to be absorbed before a new product can be launched. I'm afraid the source of the raw material is not a selling point when Artemis talc eventually reaches housewives in Sydney or San Francisco. But I like the idea, and the name. Now, are we agreed, provided our lawyers do what they're paid for? I never allow legal advisers to be present at meetings of this kind. They beaver away at making everything impossible. My objective is the reverse – to make things possible.'

'I've already explained to Quentin.' Charlie leaned forward, his hands on his knees. 'Under Scots Law we give you what is known as a 'feu'. You pay me a purely nominal 'feu duty', but it really means that you became the freeholder.'

'I should add', said Quentin, 'that while Mr McLeish remains the feudal superior, you became his vassal in respect of your interest. I thought you'd like that.'

'Do I have to do homage?' Sacher was intrigued by the anachronism. It had an imperial ring that appealed to him.

'One further thing.' Charlie spoke with increasing diffidence. 'My father's Will laid down that my brother had to give his consent to any disposal of this kind.' Quentin knew what it cost Charlie to make this admission. There was an immediate cooling. The atmosphere had become tense. The silence was broken only by Sacher's personal Morse Code as he tapped the table with his gold pencil.

'I did not realise until this morning, Mr McLeish, that David McLeish was your brother.' Measured civility had replaced his earlier bonhomie. 'Nor did I appreciate until this moment that he was in any way involved in our business together. I hope it will not be necessary to carry out fresh negotiations with him, because frankly my time is limited. Are you in a position to say what your brother's attitude will be?'

158

'I can look after that.' Quentin sprang in before Charlie could ruin the whole consensus. 'I will obtain David's agreement before the evening is over. I suggest we proceed on that basis.'

'If you say so, Quentin.' Sacher looked doubtful. For a moment he seemed lost in thought. Then he let the pencil, balanced on its point, drop. The sharp report signalled the end of the discussion. 'In that case it's settled. We can spend the rest of the day enjoying the attractions of this delightful city.' He rose to stand facing the window. 'I will confess to one disappointment. Your Castle. Look at it.'

Faced with this unexpected heresy they turned their eyes obediently to the west side of the fortress.

'It looks like a tenement, or the barrack building which I suppose it is.' Sacher dismissed it with a wave.

'What you're seeing', Charlie replied, are in fact the Army Quarters. They were built very much later than the historic parts of the Castle which are invisible from this angle.'

'You should see the other side,' Fiona exclaimed. 'The drawbridge and the Esplanade where they hold the Tattoo.'

'I would appreciate the privilege of seeing that. Unfortunately there is no time.'

'Oh, but there is. The Tattoo starts at ten o'clock. You could be there and still be in plenty of time for the reception in the Assembly Rooms.'

'I imagine there are no reservations available at such short notice.' He showed no sign of taking her offer seriously.

'Mr Sacher, you will be given a seat in the V.I.P. Box. If I can arrange it, will you come with me?'

He hesitated for only a second.

'I would be honoured.'

'There's something strange about this,' Quentin and Houlihan were gathering up their papers. Sacher was already on the telephone. The others had left. 'I did not detect any trace of the giant computer. Don't tell me the omiscient eye was closed.'

'You got it in one.' Houlihan tapped the side of his nose

159

confidentially. 'I gave him the abstract before you arrived. Sam had made his mind up and he was sweet on the Highland girl. That was okay. So he was no trouble. But if that other McLeish blows the deal you'll see nothing but Hermes' vapour trail.'

Fiona and Charlie had reached the mezzanine floor when Quentin caught up with them.

'Just how are you going to get the seats for the Tattoo?', he asked. 'As if I didn't know.'

'General Havvy will do it. I've never asked him for anything before'

'I expect he will. If there are no spare seats the Sappers will be ordered to build an extension for you. That was very clever, and Houlihan's delighted. But watch out. The shapely praying mantis in the person of Signorina Liberta won't be wildly keen to see our Samuel deserting her reception – even temporarily.'

'I'll get him back in good time. Quentin,' she laid her hand on his arm, 'there's dancing tonight. Will you dance with me?'

'If I get the chance.'

'You will.'

'Would you mind explaining', Charlie halted, grasping the handrail, 'how you think you're going to get my sympathetic brother to agree? I'm not being funny, God knows. Why should he help me now? He has always refused to do so in the past.'

'I have an idea he may not be so awkward as you think.' It was essential to sustain Charlie's morale. 'He has other problems too.'

'I doubt it. This is devilish awkward. We don't want a scene in public. But if he doesn't play at once, it's clear that Uncle Sam will withdraw his offer. Do you want me to join you and have it out with him?'

'Not yet. I'll let you know.'

'In that case I'm going to toddle along Princes Street to the New Club for a glass of whisky before we change for the horrors that lie ahead. Care to come?'

'No thanks. I've got some telephoning to do.'

'Claude, I want to hear the sweet voice of reason.' Quentin gave his senior partner a résumé of the Sacher conclave.

'Sounds as though you've kept the ball rolling.'

'I'm not optimistic. Up against beastly David once more. Every time we try to get out of the maze we end up in the centre.'

'I know all the paths but I will never get to Cordoba.'

'Very oracular, but not very helpful. We've had one brush with D. McLeish already. Not promising for the main event. And I've had to say we'll get his consent today.'

'And how, dear boy, will you do that?'

'Charlie's a broken reed, but I'm quite keen to face David and get under that thick skin of his. I thought we might bluff him. Threaten him with going to court on the grounds that he's abusing the intentions of his father as testator. He won't like the publicity.'

'I can't see that working. Even eyeball to eyeball. Something more oblique is needed. I say, you're not getting too involved, are you – I mean personally?'

No reflection about the unexpected meeting with his brother at the Lorraine worried David. He had already dismissed the incident from his mind when he passed through the Doric pillars of the Royal Scottish Academy. Preliminary soundings about the Barleycorn Trust had, his Area Manager assured him over lunch, gone well, and now Sir Atholl Dunnet, the President of the Academy, received him affably. The President would be happy to cooperate with the Trust, but he was anxious to carry his colleagues with him. Some of them were chary about sponsorship; and therefore he had asked one or two of the most influential to dine with him that evening. If David could join them, he was confident that they would find they were all of the same opinion.

'I'm most grateful to you, Sir Atholl. I'll look forward to it.'

As David walked up the Royal Mile, he felt an upsurge of excitement within him – partly due the good will of Sir Atholl, and the knowledge that the Barleycorn Trust seemed to be heading for success, but more attributable to the fact that he had an assignation with Bianca.

For most of the afternoon he had felt she was with him. Her face on posters advertising *Daughter of Poppaea*, or on blown-up photographs and labels earing the name of Aphrodite cosmetics, had followed him the length of Princes Street. Each time he looked in a shop window she was there. One ingenious mirror arrangement carried so many likenesses that her lips palpably moved, as in an early bioscope. Aphrodite's representative had been busy. There were few corners without Bianca.

'O Timballoo! How happy we are
When we live in a Sieve and a crockery-jar!'

Repeating to himself Lear's rhyme from 'The Jumblies', he paid his fee for entry to the Castle, and climbed the cobbled hill through Foog's Gate. He found her at the Half Moon Battery, surrounded by photographers and T.V. crews. Perched on the balustrade, she arranged her tartan plaid in folds, faced into the breeze, and pointed towards Princes Street. A series of poses were needed before the cameramen were satisfied.

'Mr McLeish! What a pleasant surprise.' She made an excuse to escape from the more persistent reporters.

'I happened to be passing.' He made a token bow.

'Such an obvious route. Won't the press recognise you? Aren't you embarrassed?'

'Let me show you I'm not. Can I kiss you?'

'In front of all these cameras? You're mad. Deliciously mad, but mad. Where have you been?'

He told her about his meeting with Sir Atholl and his dinner engagement.

'That is more like the wise David who impresses everyone. I somehow think that dinner *chez* Sam would not be a good idea for you. But you must come to the reception as my guest. I've had the most marvellous day. Beautiful tour of the Castle. I've seen St Margaret's Chapel and the Crown Jewels – the Honours of Scotland, as they're called here. I like that as a name. I like it all.' She embraced the Castle with an enormous sweeping

162

gesture. He covered her hand when it came to rest on the coping stone. She entwined their fingers.

'I'll give a great party when we announce the Barleycorn Trust. Will you come and bless it?' The prospect of Bianca as his permanent hostess entranced him.

'I will, if I can.'

'And . . .'.

She put a finger to his lips. 'You're not to say anything more just now.'

'You mean Sacher? The emperor is not lightly mocked – but he's going to be.'

'David, you must understand. We have a saying in Italy that it's better to have a dead cat in your bed than a woman from Lucca. I'd be like the Lucchese for you just now. Does that shock you? Sam's my boss since you sold Aphro. And there's another contract. He's behind my next film.' The car was waiting for her. 'I've got to be photographed at Stevenson's house. Part of the pre-publicity. Then I've got to change. But there will, there must be time eventually. Why don't you come to Rome next week?'

Left to himself, David started a leisurely descent. He stopped at the ancient bombard known as Mons Meg, and the pile of huge stone cannon balls. Today he could lift one of them and load the massive piece of ordnance. He gave it a friendly tap as he turned away.

Chapter XV

There was a deceptive lull as Sam Sacher received his dinner
guests with cordiality and lethal Martinis. Bianca would join
them as soon as she had escaped from her routine appearance
at the cinema where *Poppaea* was being unveiled. Much to
Quentin's surprise, there was no question of their having to sit
through the film. The reception was the place where points
could be scored and where Bianca would hold court.

'Quentin,' Kirsty took him by the arm, 'I don't like it.
Charlie's wandering round in a daze. What's happened?'

'All was peace this afternoon.' From the nervous tremor in
her voice, some reassurance was needed.

'He said that Fiona landed Mr Sacher without having to use
a net. But that won't do by itself. He's convinced that David will
sabotage it. Do we really need his consent?'

'We can't get hold of the wretched Will, but it would be futile
to think we can go ahead without him. Anyhow, you know it's
his agreement that Charlie wants – much more than the contract.'

'My poor Charlie, beating his head against an iceberg.'

'You mustn't despair. We're not beaten yet. David's here in
Edinburgh. Did Charlie tell you we met him at lunch?'

'No!' Quentin gave her an edited version of the encounter,
and Charlie's reaction. 'That explains it. He's too proud to say
he's been affronted again. We would do far better to go back to
Skye and forget all about selling the Loch. The anguish will be

too much for him.'

'Listen carefully – we'll have to join the others in a minute. David is coming to the reception after dinner. Bianca asked him. I'm going to take him on. This goes far beyond normal professional behaviour, but I don't care. I'll say with all the force I can muster that he has no conceivable reason to frustrate the deal. It would be pure bloody-mindedness. It doesn't affect him financially, as your sons will inherit after Charlie. If he says no it will be nothing but malice, and I will make certain – as I will warn him – that everyone he knows learns that the generous promoter of the Barleycorn Trust has fouled his own nest.'

'Quentin, my dear, he knows – or will know – that our share of the money will be invested in the Estate, and he hates the thought of Charlie having the funds to do that. He wants us to go down on bended knee, preferably in public, and admit that we were wrong, that his father's feudal fancies were all poppycock. I suppose he would also like me to say that I made a mistake in rejecting him for Charlie. Don't look so violent.'

'Sorry, but that's no way to behave. It's psychopathic.'

'Maybe it is. But I know what has to be done. There's only one person who can do it. He can have his act of penitence. I'm very willing to abase myself if it will get rid of this dreadful thing that hangs over us.'

'Do you really want to humiliate yourself like that? It will be quite hellish.'

'I've always known I'd have to do it. Thank heaven there's not long to wait. I might take fright! Will you make sure that I get a chance to speak to him before Charlie does?'

'Wasn't there a Scottish heroine who kept the enemy at bay by barring the door with her own arm?'

'Yes. Kate Barlas. I've not lived all these years at The Keep for nothing.'

Bianca swept into the room in flame-coloured chiffon and an extravagant diamond necklace, and the party moved downstairs to the restaurant. Sacher asked Kirsty and Signora Montone to sit on either side of him. He took some pains with the

165

seating plan. It was a conventional one, and no one's susceptibilities could be offended, but the pattern did not reflect their inner thoughts. It was impossible not to be aware of an air of premonition. They were all, for their own reasons, marking time.

Kirsty, a gracious adornment to anyone's dinner table, might be engaging Sacher with her account of the tribal ceremonies at The Keep, but Quentin knew from her occasional glances at him and from the anxious way she looked towards her husband that her mind was elsewhere. Fiona caught his eye as often as she dared to look across the table. He had already said that her blue and green dress befitted her water-sprite image: now she looked like an elverine. She was listening to Houlihan's colourful tale of his exploits at skeet-shooting, a relaxation he enjoyed in the States, but the challenge in her expression was, he knew, for him.

To continue the contrapuntal arrangement, Sacher, a genial and attentive host, could not refrain from gazing intermittently at Bianca. He was trying to establish a bond, however tenuous, between them. Bianca, who could not have been unaware of Sacher's signals, spoke most frequently to Charlie. Did he think Skye would be a good place to shoot the Scottish scenes in her new film? Charlie replied politely that the story was, as its name implied, set on the Solway coast where the scenery was less rugged than on the Island. Skye would not be an authentic setting. Never easy to read, Charlie appeared intent on keeping his worries to himself.

If he was not on form, there was still something pathetically dignified about him. He was like a beached mammal. Quentin remembered the film director who could not make up his mind whether Moby Dick was the whale or the man. But it was not only his size that separated Charlie from the others. The Pirelli-like Houlihan's skin appeared distended at high pneumatic pressure. Charlie had more than bulk. He had his own persona, something that no one could reach.

Signora Montone had lost something of her earlier verve, and she too looked thoughtfully at Charlie from time to time.

Quentin asked if she had a family link with the famous *condottiere* Braccio da Montone, the ruler of Perugia. Did her husband follow the banner of the Montone, the black ram? No. He had no connection with Perugia. There was a family tree in his study, but it did not record a *condottiere*. As if to discourage further enquiries, she observed that Mr Lawrence was a very knowledgeable, very erudite person. Was that, looking in Fiona's direction, always an advantage?

The atmosphere was becoming oppressive. Quentin wanted to stand up, clap his hands, and cause a diversion. Sacher seemed to have the same thought. Seeking to draw Charlie into the general conversation, he asked if the restaurant had any particular claim to fame. Charlie roused himself to recall that it had featured in one of Eric Linklater's novels. The author, he chuckled at the memory, had described the dining room crowded with revellers after a Calcutta Cup match at Murrayfield. The saxophonist had left his seat with the band to wander, still playing, among the tables. An over-refreshed diner had emptied a box of snuff into the ululating instrument, and Linklater had written an epic account of the consequent, concerted sneezing.

'I like that,' Sacher called out. 'I've been to many dinners that should have been snuffed out. But the saxophone has always had a special place in our family.'

'I didn't know you had any musical talent.' Bianca laughed at this unexpected revelation.

'Not for its sound. It was invented by a Belgian called Adolphe Sax. But he went bankrupt and my father used to hold him up as an example of what happened to anyone who failed to market the product. 'Remember the saxophone,' he'd say when he was presented with an unsatisfactory balance sheet.'

'Sam,' Bianca pouted, 'just for once stop thinking about your percentage point!'

'It makes its own music. But I see Fiona is getting restless.'

'I think we should go,' she replied gratefully. 'We have to be in our places before the Tattoo starts.'

Bianca had the last word as the dinner party broke up.

'Don't let him put in a bid for the Castle, Fiona. If he has it shipped stone by stone to Long Island, the Rock left behind will look too bald. Besides, he has his own great palazzo there, all ready for occupation. Haven't you, Sam?'

'Such luxury.' Fiona kicked off her shoes to sink her toes in the deep pile of the carpet. The Sacher limousine sped along Princes Street and up the Mound. 'You only appreciate it in contrast to what happens every day. That's something you wouldn't know about, Mr Sacher.'

'I reckon we take too many things for granted. Not enough time to think about them. Time takes on new dimensions when you've got a world-wide corporation to look after.'

'Time. Wait.' She fished in her handbag and brought out a diamond-shaped traffic pass. 'That's to go on the windscreen.'

'What does it say?' Sam read the typescript on the back. Signed by the Chief Constable, it adjured the City Police to allow Miss Fiona McDhuie to pass without hindrance. He gave it to the driver. 'I'm impressed by your skill at manipulation – as I was this afternoon, Fiona. And please call me Sam.'

The car drew up at the entrance to the V.I.P. Stand. A subaltern wearing the Red Hackle of the Black Watch in his bonnet escorted them to their seats. General Havvy greeted Fiona with a kiss, shook hands with Sacher, and presented them to the G.O.C. They're like children who've been deep-frozen years ago, Fiona thought, as the introductions were made with a nice regard for protocol. General Havvy, as the junior kind of General, punctiliously addressed the G.O.C. as 'Sir'. He wore the dark-green and black uniform of the Royal Green Jackets, whose Regimental Colonel he was. With his white hair and moustache, and features refined by age, he offered a sharp contrast to the more muscular figure of his younger, but superior, officer in his scarlet mess kit.

'How did you do it?' whispered Fiona, seated next to him.

'Said it was still a secret, but he was likely to be the next American Ambassador to the Court of St James. Why shouldn't he? I expect he's got enough Red Indian blood in him. As long as he doesn't start slanging his President, we should be all right. But remember, I want another day on the Borve next year, if I'm spared.'

The G.O.C. was explaining the structure of the pibroch – the *urlar*, the original melody, followed by variations which the piper elaborated with grace notes played ever more quickly before returning to the main theme in slow time. Sacher listened and watched with evident interest as the programme unfolded. There were contingents from the Bersaglieri doubling to their trumpet, the Royal Danish Guards in red tunics and bearskins, and General Havvy's own Green Jackets who provided the drill display – all performing for their pleasure.

'Who are these guys in the bleachers?', he asked. 'They must be pretty cold.'

'The Festival visitors, may they rest in peace,' the G.O.C. replied. 'You're dead right. It is cold out there. They don't have electric fires or a canopy to keep the rain off, as we have. But it doesn't deter them. The public stands – bare boards on top of scaffolding – are always full.'

'They certainly seem to be enjoying themselves. I like the way the commentator stirs them up.'

'He's also the producer. He's excellent at getting the audience to identify with those taking part, with individual regiments.'

'I've been to Annapolis, but it's nothing like this. Much more impersonal. You've got three aspects – historical, theatrical and military – all combined. That's what does it.'

Sam was lost in thought. He might have been calculating how this tripartite information could be fed into the computer.

Despite the presence of so many foreign troops, it was essentially a Scottish evening. In addition to the Highland dancing, the main tableau showing an event from the past had a Scottish subject. It portrayed the last scene at the siege of Lucknow during the Mutiny. The survivors in the besieged garrison fired occasional shots to keep up morale in face of the sepoys surrounding them. Then a tattered nurse – the nanny to one of the officers' families, according to the programme – ran frantically round the wall of the redoubt. As she climbed the rampart she screamed 'Can ye no hear them? Can ye no hear them?' Enraged at the officer's lack of understanding, she beat him repeatedly on the chest with her fists before a couple of weary soldiers led her away. The silence when they resumed their posts was broken only by the crunching of boots and odd bursts of rifle fire. They peered into the half-light, but there was nothing to be seen. Then a shrill, reedy sound, barely audible, came from the distance. It grew louder; it gradually merged with the beat of the drum. It reached a crescendo as Sir Colin Campbell's Argylls marched into the arena to relieve the fortress. As a good Scotswoman born in the glens – if the legend was to be believed – the nanny had heard the rescuing pipes long before anyone else.

'I begin to see', said Sacher after they had made their goodbyes, 'why the lochans, as you call them, and the Isle of Skye are so important to you. That bit of play-acting we've just seen means that only Scots can understand the Scots. There's something about all this I don't follow, but I'm trying.' He smiled delightedly as they drove down Castle Wynd.

'Can I ask you something, Sam? I want to consult Zeus. You own a chain of hotels. If I give you all the statistics about our tiny place – all the occupancy rates, types of visitor, the facilities we offer – will you have them programmed, and tell me what we're doing wrong?'

'Zeus is omnipotent, but I fear you're really too small for him. Let me make another suggestion. When do you graduate at your university?'

'Next June.'

'If you want a job, and if you'll leave your Island for a little, I'll give you a year in my office. You can see how it all works, and then come back to Scotland, unless you change your mind.'

'I think I'd like that very much. You're much too kind. Can I tell you nearer the time?' She was touched by his thoughtfulness. If other things went wrong, it might be a solution.

'Of course.'

Chapter XVI

All was well in David's world as he entered the flower-decked entrance hall of the Assembly rooms. Sir Atholl Dunnet's port and the Academicians' enthusiasm for the Trust both contributed to his sense of well-being, and now he had a rendez-vous with Bianca. He was upset to be accosted by a drunk in the cloakroom. Drying his hands on the Towelmaster, he turned at the noise of retching behind him. The bedraggled figure who had been vomiting in the handbasin peered at him through bloodshot eyes.

'Another bleeding Festival visitor.' He stood up unsteadily. 'Come to throw buns to the natives?'

Aware that a sober person is always at a disadvantage argu-ing with an inebriate, David made to leave, but the drunk barred his way.

'Want to see how the Picts live? Is that it?' Rocking on his heels, he prodded David's chest with a grubby finger. 'Why don't you piss off?'

'You're mistaken.' David pushed his hand aside.

'You think I'm a drunken Scot looking at the Thistle. It's the toffee-nosed, patronising English that make me spew. Not the whisky.'

'I'm as much of a Scotsman as you are,' David said coldly. 'Now, if you'll let me pass.'

'Oh you are, are you? As much of a Scotsman.' He mimicked him. 'Well, you don't bloody well speak like one. I'll tell you

171

what you are.' He lunged forward. 'You're a fancy man. A poor dressed-up poof. A Laird's son too, I'll be bound. We've had your sort ever since the Clearances. You drove us off for sheep. Woe to thee, O land, the great sheep is here! But our day's coming, and you won't be able to kiss my arse. It's coming yet. It's coming yet, for a' that.' He staggered back to the basin.

David was shaken. He looked at the heaving shoulders. Despite his drunken mutterings, this was an educated man. He had quoted three poets. David was tempted to take him to task and explain what he did. But it would do no good. He wouldn't be believed, and he wasn't going to have his evening spoiled.

He could not at first find Bianca, but from past experience – he had addressed the Annual meeting of the Scottish Whisky Association there last year – he knew the geography of the building. There were two large public rooms connected by a central concourse. In one of them the hungry guests, their appetites whetted by watching the orgies in '*Poppaea*', were attacking the cold buffet. The Sacher party, replete with the Caledonian Hotel's rich viands, were unlikely to be among the avid consumers. In the second room a steel band – white teeth, dark skins and multi-coloured blouses – improbably played before the high mirrors, now, alas, speckled with age. The dusty chandeliers cast a pale glimmer of light over the crowded floor. Edging round the dancers, David made for the small drawing room at the end of the main salon. It often sheltered the top brass. The entrance was guarded by two formidable bouncers, but Bianca caught sight of him and her wave was enough to allow him entry.

'Hullo, David,' Quentin interrupted him. 'How fares the Barleycorn? Still whipping in the breeze, I hope.'

'Couldn't be better. They're going to swear an oath of allegiance to the Trust. I'll tell you about it, but I'd better find my hostess.' He faltered as he saw who was standing beside Bianca, but it was too late to withdraw.

'David, darling,' She greeted him. 'Look, I've got both McLeishes together at last. Your brother's been telling me everything that happens on that marvellous Island you're so

172

reticent about.'

'Charlie,' his expression was studiedly neutral, 'this is a surprise.'

'Not for me. I knew you were coming.'

Quentin waited, ready to intervene. The brothers loured at each other like hostile stags. To Quentin's eye they appeared in high relief, leaving those around on a different plane. The family affinity was more marked when they stood face to face – the same arrogant bearing, accentuated by the angle at which David tilted his chin, modified by Charlie's resigned demeanour: in all, more than enough to point to their common ancestry. Their clothes showed the same resemblance and minor differences. Well-cut dinner jackets, but David's was sharper, more flared. Charlie's was stretched under the arms, but his waistcoat of McLeish tartan had its own élan. In silence they were taking each other's measure. Time had momentarily stopped.

'Well,' turning to Bianca, David was the first to speak, 'I'm glad someone's pleased to see me. I got a very dubious welcome downstairs. Not from the most attractive of our fellow-countrymen, I admit.' He could by now affect amusement at the drunk's abuse. 'I was accused of being a renegade.'

'True, isn't it?' Charlie had found his voice.

'I don't follow.' The cold light in his eyes contradicted the smile lingering on his mouth.

'Wha will be a traitor knave? A song you've conveniently forgotten.' Feet apart, thumbs in his waistcoat, Charlie held his ground.

'David, how many years?' Kirsty, heaven-sent, swooped between them.

'Kirsty!' David took her hand in both of his. 'Not a day older.'

'You're so gallant! Aren't you going to dance with me?'

'My pleasure.' It would have taken someone even more insensitive than David to decline the invitation. They went off arm-in-arm.

173

'Steady, *mon brave.*' Quentin had to restrain Charlie who showed signs of following them. 'That was a false move.'

'He's come to sneer at us. I'll gralloch him. And Kirsty . . .'

'Will bring him back in a different frame of mind. He's probably as annoyed as you. Your remark wasn't exactly an olive branch. Now Signora Montone's making signs that she wants to talk to you. Go and join her on the sofa.'

It had been a near thing. Kirsty had almost lost her chance. Quentin watched them on the dance floor. David had an old-fashioned way of moving. Elegant, slightly stiff, his steps were precise. He was well within himself. He had rationalised dancing, like everything else. But Kirsty was pleading the cause of her emotional, extrovert husband. Would David recognise that his own analytical approach could at times be repellent, that there was room for some concession? Or would he see in Kirsty's appealing to him an admission that she had been wrong, years ago, in choosing Charlie? It was hard to say.

For himself, Quentin felt in limbo. Despite his groundwork, it was clear that there were limits to what could be achieved by refining the arguments and presenting the problem as he saw it. The issue lay between two brothers who originally had more in common than they would admit. They both wanted to succeed, to be in charge, to tell people what to do, but as they followed divergent paths their endemic defects had become magnified, with unhappy results. Quentin wondered whether there was a mathematical formula to merge their virtues and eliminate their vices. Probably not, but a median course, one he would choose himself, was the only sane basis for the good life. He would not pretend that this was enough. He would not be content to be protected by the scepticism for which David had chided him. He needed Fiona's grace, her very personal intuition, to complement his intellectual judgment. He looked round the room for her, but she had not returned from the Castle. Anyhow, these musings were irrelevant. The climax was being enacted on the floor.

'You look so happy, David.'

'From seeing you again. You're still the Wren I used to take out to dinner. Not a trace of grey hair. It's uncanny.'

'Don't inspect too closely. But you're not only sleek and prosperous. You seem more contented. Are you?'

'As much as anyone can be.' The thought of Bianca made him regard Kirsty with even more affection.

'I think I know the reason. Will you tell me, yourself?'

'You'll be the first to know.' He was moved, as he always had been, by her ability to read his mind. 'When, or more accurately, if.'

'No change. Always meticulous. David, I want to talk about Charlie. He's not well. I'm afraid he's losing control.'

'I'm sorry. I really am.'

'I know. Though he wouldn't believe you. I wish – you know what I wish. There need never have been this distance between you.'

'That from you, my dear, is mildly ingenuous.'

'Will you do something for me?'

'Did I ever deny you anything?' In the evening's euphoria he could afford a friendly gesture – which she probably had in mind – despite Charlie's gaucheness.

'Not unless it inconvenienced you,' she laughed nervously, and this won't. It's why we're here.' She hurried over her words. 'Loch Dhuie is said to be full of diatomite. It's valuable, and Sacher is willing to pay a huge price for it. But Charlie thinks he may need your consent under the Will, and he won't go ahead unless you agree.'

'What a remarkable find!' He stopped in the middle of the floor. 'Dollars in Loch Dhuie.' He laughed. 'Cash registers clicking over the corries.'

'It's not just the money.' She recognised David's quizzical expression – it could conceal something cold and clinical. 'Though that would be useful now that the whisky's gone sour.'

'Will you believe me that there was nothing I could do for Old Portree?'

'Yes, I will. But selling the Loch couldn't affect you. It's your agreement, your recognition that he's done a good job. That's

175

all he thinks about.'

'Charlie's still the lucky one. To have you to ask for him.'

'He doesn't know about this. Will you help, David?'

'It goes against what I believe in. I don't hate Charlie, though he thinks I do. What I hated was seeing the eager way he sank himself – and you – in the McLeish Mausoleum, in keeping alive all the obsolete tomfoolery that our father taught him. You can't immure yourself in the past to such an extent that it engulfs your whole being.'

'That's not fair. You know he runs the Estate well.'

'But it's always heading backwards. He's weaving his own shroud. When you married him I decided to get out of the bog once and for all. To live in the future. You know all the rest.'

'I'd hoped for a more friendly reply.'

'My dear.' He saw he had been too bitter. 'Of course I won't stop this diatomite thing. I've only an accidental legal interest at best. It would be illogical of me to interfere, and you know', he smiled down at her, 'how I hate being illogical.'

'That sounds like you.'

'But I make one condition. Your sons, my nephews, will be the real beneficiaries. You must promise that they will be given every chance to lead their own lives.'

'I will. And will you say it's for him? For all the long line of McLeishes? Don't let him think it's just for me.'

'I will say I look on it as an investment in a progressive future.'

'David,' She clung against him in her relief, 'I could kiss you if it wouldn't be misunderstood.'

'You could still try.'

The heightened colour in Kirsty's cheek told Quentin what he wanted to know.

'He's agreed,' she greeted him. 'He's a generous person at heart. She squeezed David's arm.

'I see,' said David. 'This is a put-up job. Does it come within your professional brief?'

'I'm not sure,' Quentin replied, 'but I thought you'd see

sense. To be blunt, you'd have to be a four-letter man not to. Let's have a drink on it.' He still had a role as croupier. They must accept that their new-found harmony was real before telling Charlie.

'Was it his idea, Kirsty?' David asked while Quentin fought his way to the bar. 'I'd like to think it was yours.'

'We both thought of it. He told me what was at stake, but I knew I had to speak to you myself.'

'As a failed Don,' Quentin brought the drinks, 'can I be allowed to say that you have come to a Homeric decision? Like the great scene in the *Iliad*?'

'I'm not sure I'm with you.' David looked perplexed.

'I'm certainly not.'

'I won't bore you with the build-up, but you remember when Achilles has slain Hector, the aged Priam beseeches him not to mutilate his son's corpse, as was their merry custom. Achilles feels his wrath is appeased with Hector's death, so he lets Priam claim the body – and that was thought to have been a great, heroic thing for Achilles to have done. Not to push it too far, I see a parallel with your agreement just now.'

'Achilles was never my favourite man, but I'm flattered.'

'On the plane, when you enthused about your Barleycorn scheme, I knew there were embers beneath your frosty exterior. That's really rather a nice thing to say.'

'Yes, it is. I hope Charlie will see it like that. Slainthè.

The Achilles witticism was soon to turn to ashes. While the triumphant trio were intent on their dram, Charlie and Signora Montone were talking of other, far-off things.

'Beatrice!'

'Carlo, *carissimo*. This is absurd!'

'When did you recognise me?'

'When Bianca told me about David she mentioned that he had a brother. As soon as I saw David this morning I knew it was going to be you. And I remembered your name, *tesoro* – although you never said goodbye or wrote to me. You just left me on the beach at Riccione.'

177

Charlie shook himself. He found it difficult to throw his mind back so many years, to recall a wartime *affaire*.

'A long time ago. It was simpler then – and agreeable.'

'Thank you, Carlo. I know that compliments never came easily from you and they usually had a double meaning. Do you remember the races at Ravenna?'

'We drank too much gin after the Alexander Stakes.'

'You had two captured horses you were going to enter. You said you would call one of them Dante's Joy, in my honour, and you let me choose. I loved the chestnut – and he won.'

'By a couple of lengths from the Ninth Lancers. You collected the cup for me.'

'Then I found out that you'd named the horse after the favourite in the English Derby, and not after me at all. It wasn't kind.'

'Have you still got the Villa?'

'We sold it a long time ago. Riccione's full of tourists now.'

'What happened to the Giardino del Bosco?'

'I don't know. It's probably a discothèque. No more spumante beneath the oleanders on the terrace. No more moonlight bathing.'

'In the nude, on horseback.' He sighed at the recollection.

'Thinking about it is not good for us, particularly at our age. We're mature, responsible, respectable. And you have a most charming wife. You must be very happy.'

'Why wouldn't you let her know that we have met before? I caught your sign, but only just. Kirsty wouldn't be annoyed. It's a long time ago, and I wasn't married when I knew you. She's very understanding.'

'She's sympathetic. I could see that.'

'She'd be more amused than anything.'

'Wiser to leave memories like that undisturbed. I often thought about you after these days, but I never thought of telling my husband. Whatever I said, Egidio would have wondered and wondered. It would not have done anyone any good. Charlie, I have to tell you, there is another reason for my speaking to you now.'

178

'Yes?' He followed her eyes towards Bianca and back again.
'She's our daughter.'

'Our daughter? Good God.' He stammered at the shock.

'I thought you might have guessed.'

'You're sure?' He looked searchingly at her. He was fairly certain that in that long, hot summer he had not been the only one dipping in the powder keg, and he had left a whole regiment of randy officers behind.

'Quite certain. Don't you remember I spend three months at the Villa before you disappeared – and Egidio was still in Bologna?'

'And no one knows?' He sounded doubtful.

'No one.' She laid an affectionate hand on his arm. 'But I had to tell you –if only for one reason. Bianca likes your brother, and he wants to marry her.'

'Marry her? David?' Charlie started to laugh, a harsh, hoarse laughter. 'That's good. That's wonderful. That's priceless!' His laughter redoubled. He brushed tears from his eyes.

'Carlo! Stop it!' He started to cough. He rose unsteadily, fighting for breath.

'Charlie!' David hurried up to him. 'I'm all for it. I'm not going to stand in your way. What's the matter, old boy?'

'You're. . . ?' His lips parted in a grin, but the question was unfinished. David leapt to catch him as he collapsed on the sofa. His eyes were glazed and he fell on one side.

'Get a doctor!' David knelt beside him. He turned him onto his back, placed the palms of his hands on his brother's chest and leaned with the full weight of his body. Three times he pressed, then putting his mouth to Charlie's he tried to inflate his lungs. But there was no response. Charlie was no longer capable of adjusting to adversity.

Did it really need a coronary to bring them together? that was the thought which struck Quentin then, and for long after. He was also to remember the silent scene – Kirsty numbed, impassive, as though watching a mime; Fiona, who had just arrived, putting a protective arm round her; Signora Montone sobbing uncontrollably. Only Sacher and Houlihan seemed able to move. They went in search of assistance, but they and the others knew it was an empty quest.

A doctor was found. He needed only a brief examination.

'He's dead.' He stood up. 'It looks like a coronary. Has he had any symptoms? Any previous record?'

Seeing that Kirsty was not capable of speaking, Fiona answered.

'About ten days ago. He had a mild attack.'

'Have there been any signs of lassitude? Has he looked a bit under the weather?'

Kirsty and Fiona both nodded.

'Almost certainly a coronary. It would be nearly instantaneous.'

His impersonal tone had a calming effect. Reality began to reassert itself, but it was David who took charge. Calmly purposeful, he gave instructions to the St Andrew's Ambulance men who came with a stretcher.

'Kirsty,' he said quietly, 'There's nothing I, or anyone else can say that will be of help to you. But he must have seen that we were at one about what worried him. Hold on to that. And there are worse ways to go. He wouldn't suffer.' He would take Kirsty and Fiona back to the Caledonian and Signora Montone would go with them. Would Quentin ring the Manager to say what had happened? Sacher's offer of his suite was declined, but they would stay in the Hotel until arrangements were made for the long journey to The Keep.

As they left, Fiona looked anxiously at Quentin. She seemed about to speak. She moved her hand tentatively towards him, then dropped it. She followed the others.

Signora Montone would not let Bianca accompany her, adding almost with asperity that she had her public duty to perform. There were still people waiting to meet her.

Another hour was needed before the manumission of admirers was complete. Leaving the Assembly Rooms, Sacher noticed an Aphrodite display on the staircase.

'Last year's placards. They'll have to do better than that,' he

180

said ominously.

'Sam! Not now.'

'That was deliberate. Never forget, my dear, that the diurnal round – that was my father's phrase – goes on. When you're upset there's much to be said for keeping that in mind.'

'Yes. We're professionals.'

When they reached the Hotel, Quentin assured Sacher that, despite the evening's unhappy experience, the diatomite contract could be regarded as settled. He had David's word that he would cooperate, and there was no reason to expect dissent from Charlie's executors.

'Sure, I understand. It seems very trivial tonight, but that will pass, and it's a good deal for that wretched man's family. I'll say goodbye. I leave in a few hours' time. One thing I'm certain of, Mr Unobtrusive Quentin. You're going to remain my merchant banker in this country. Give my regards to Claude Albizzi.'s

'Goodbye, Quentin.' Bianca shook his hand. 'I don't know when I'll see you again. Mamma and I are flying to Rome in the morning. They want me for a film conference. No rest, you see.' She laughed nervously.

'Then,' Sacher added, 'I hope she'll make an early and prolonged trip to the States.'

Houlihan stayed behind to take his own farewell. Though normally resilient, he showed signs of being shaken by the night's events.

'I'd best be going now. I'm sorry about that poor guy. I'd only just met him. Anyway I gotta say thanks to you and your girlfriend. It was a good job. Sam's still got his options open, and pretty soon there'll be the Atlantic ocean between them.'

Chapter XVII

Quentin got his key from the Reception Desk. As he paced the silent corridor to his room at the far end he was tempted to ring Claude. Waking him up would be a fair return for the strain he had caused since he launched the McLeish exercise. It was easy to imagine how quickly he would identify the dramatic elements in the last act. 'As leaves on the tree, so is the life of man.' He would add abruptly that Albizzi's function was now discharged. There would be other flippant comments, and Quentin was not in the mood to relish his partner's worldly wisdom, his innate irreverence. He had deployed his talents as best he could on behalf of his clients. Although the outcome had been marred by tragedy, that could not be foreseen, and a resigned acceptance was in order. He was his own man.

He had passed the Sacher party's doors. How would they remember the night's dénouement?

The Protean Sam was probably the most predictable. There was a lively, generous spirit behind his awesome manner, but any thought of Loch Dhuie would soon be submerged beneath his global activities. By a quirk of fate he had witnessed, and to some extent occasioned, the final fraternal joust. Now he would resume orbit. Like Bacon's men in high places he was at once the servant of fame and business. He was returning to his own mythological world of Hermes girdling the earth and Zeus, the much-enduring computer that dominated everything and everyone except its master. He had a proprietorial, if not more intimate, interest in Bianca. It was not clear how far his feelings were returned.

Bianca? There was nothing artless about her. Her career was her first concern and she knew very well what power Sacher could wield. But if she was too exacting Sam might say that he did not buy repentance so dear. She was impressed by David's effortless charisma. She might also be attracted physically. The choice, when it came, would be made after long discussion with – or probably by – Mamma.

Kirsty had achieved the reconciliation she sought, but it had come too late. The knowledge that Charlie was already living in the shadows would do no more than temper her regret at having allowed him to come to Edinburgh. She had her sons to look after, and with her inner reserves she would in time find that there was still a life to be lived at The Keep.

David was more inscrutable. While he had been barely polite to Charlie at the Lorraine, his brother had been deliberately offensive when they met in the Assembly Rooms. His agreement to Kirsty's appeal – apparently without much demurring – had been an anticlimax. Charlie's death had brought out the best in him. He had behaved like a Chief, he had acted like the Head of the McLeishes. Kirsty could rely on his support and sympathy throughout the obsequies, and in future. But he retained his infuriatingly remote aplomb, and it was hard to believe that there would be a sea-change. The pursuit of Bianca would doubtless be continued in a different setting.

In the past few days Fiona had quickened Quentin's waking thoughts. Now it was unbearably painful to think of her. He had hoped to end the evening joyfully in her company, and from her few confidences and glances at dinner he thought she shared his view. He could understand that, part-McLeish, she had been carried away by the tide of family grief. But her gesture as she left the Assembly Rooms pointed to a distance opening up between them. It said that her loyalties lay, and would remain, on the Island. He had already seen the influence that The Keep could exert.

That was not going to make him give up. He was fully

committed. He would find a pretext to return to the parish of Borve as soon as he decently could. The telephone rang.

'Quentin?'

'Yes.'

'Beatrice Montone. It is essential that I see you at once. Bianca is saying goodnight to Sam in his suite, but she may come back. Can I come to your room?'

There was no mistaking the urgency in her voice.

'Yes, of course. We're all on the same floor.'

She arrived carrying an envelope.

'Can I offer you a drink? A small whisky as a nightcap, perhaps?'

'Thank you. I need it. You will too, when you hear what I have to say. I'm sorry if I sounded hysterical on the telphone.' Quentin shook his head. 'And thank you for letting me come. May I sit down?'

He could not imagine the purpose of her visit, though it presumably concerned Bianca.

'I want to ask you a favour, and I really have no right to do so.'

'Please.'

'Will you give this letter to David McLeish? I don't want him to receive it till after we've left, but I must be certain that it will reach him.'

'That presents no problem.'

'I want you to read it.' She took up her whisky as he opened the envelope.

He read slowly, his curiosity turning to amazement, then to sympathy for those unknowingly affected. This explained the indefinable aura, the fleeting resemblance he had sometimes sensed in Bianca without being able to ascertain the reason. Conceivably it also explained why David had first been drawn to her. The courting of the film star was no longer a comedy of manners. He looked enquiringly at her.

'I'm sorry to impose this burden on you, but I had no one else to turn to. I did not think I could ask you to act as messenger without knowing what the contents were.'

184

'Who else knows?'

'You and I are the only people who are aware who Bianca's father was. David will be the third, and I hope the last.'

'You ask him to be discreet in excusing himself from Rome next week. I suppose that's really fair to Bianca?'

'There is no real alternative.' Her voice did not suggest any fragility or weakening in her resolve. 'She is very fond of David. It does not take a mother to see why. He radiates authority, which is comforting to a young girl. I think that but for this blood-relationship she might have married him. But she has her life in front of her. She'll be disappointed, but in time she'll see that it was only an interlude. Italian experience has many such interludes, Quentin, and I'll see that she doesn't suffer for too long.'

'It won't drive her straight into the prehensile hands of Sam Sacher?'

'Possibly. But so far she's been quite capable of handling him. He knows her reason for going to Rome, instead of flying off with him, is only an excuse. He's prepared to accept it, at least for the time being.'

'Shouldn't – it's an obvious question, almost a platitude – shouldn't she know who her father is?'

'Not while Egidio is alive. My husband adores her. She loves and respects him. I have no conscience about this, none at all. It would be cruel to let them know that their life over all those years was based on a lie.' She showed the first sign of being distressed. Her mouth quivered. 'This is not for us to argue about, but can't you see that it is better, far better, for David to find a reason for disengaging? He has the ability to find a way of doing it. You're not convinced?'

'Yes, I am. It's not for me to intrude.' Watching her struggle to contain her feelings he realised that, while she and Charlie had indulged in a moment of hurried pleasure, she loved her husband and her daughter. From her anxiety she had reached understanding. He thought of himself and Fiona. It was no longer desire that he felt for her, not the sensual attraction he had first experienced. He wanted to understand her, to share everything with her, and he might be too late. 'I'm sure you're right,' he said gently. 'If Bianca learned that it was almost by accident that she had been saved from incest, the outcome would be unpredictable. She might take the view that you should have told her years ago. But it's a terrible discovery for David.'

She had the air of someone who still had something to say.

'I want to be completely open with you. I told Charlie just before he died. We had recognised each other at once, and I couldn't let David know without telling him first.'

'Did that provoke the fatal attack?'

'I don't know.' She sighed. 'We won't know. All I can say is that he looked on his daughter.'

'I thought it might have been what David told him the moment before he died. You would not know that for years Charlie felt his brother despised him. This evening, without his knowledge, Kirsty persuaded David to mend the breach. He just had time to do it and the shock may have been too much. But we knew Charlie's heart was suspect. There were signs of decline in the short time I knew him.' Quentin felt it would be unjust to leave her feeling guilty. 'I believe it was a combination of all these circumstances. You have no reason to reproach yourself for what had to be done.'

After she had left it came to him. Something that had been nagging at the back of his mind. The last hideous grin on Charlie's face. It had not been a smile to acknowledge his brother's belated contrition. Its origins had been quite different. With Beatrice's revelation he had David at his mercy. Charlie had gone to join his ancestors as the final victor.

Quentin could not sleep. He dozed from time to time, but that was all. He tried fitfully to make up his mind what to say if David confided in him, as he might do. Anyone, even the caustic David, could, if he had been on the brink of incest, feel the need to share his distress. David was not young, he was not mormally of an amorous nature, and he probably thought of Bianca as his swan song. The conversation, if it took place, would be awkward.

Then he recalled another, earlier impression while he had watched David and Kirsty. They had been unmistakenly happy in each other's company. It was not impossible that in time he and Kirsty would come together, and while The Keep would belong to her sons, the Laird would be welcome. If David could mellow, the McLeishes would be a more peaceful household.

As he flailed about in bed the thought of Fiona came back most frequently, but he could not evoke a clear picture of her. He felt more certain that his link with her had been snapped. He remembered the golden colour of her skin, weathered by wind and sun; her appearance at dinner in The Keep when she had worn a little make-up to cover her freckles; her infectious ideas that bubbled up without warning; above all, her cool kiss. But it was a still-life, a reproduction he saw from a distance. The original rapport had gone.

He could make no sense of her, or anything else. He got up.

Apart from the night porter, red-eyed and stubbly, and the cleaners rhythmically hoovering, there was no one in the Hotel vestibule. Out into the damp morning air, past the Church of St John, he let himself into Princes Street Gardens. A heavy mist hung over the branches, and he could see no more than a few yards. He heard the echo of his footsteps on the stone sets of the terrace.

He reached the American War Memorial. The bronze head of the soldier, staring sightlessly towards the Castle Rock, appeared in profile. There was someone standing on the other side of the statue. He knew that auburn hair.

'Fiona!' Hands deep in pockets, her face was hidden by the turned-up collar of her tweed coat. He stretched out his arm and drew her to him. She rubbed her cheek against his chest.

'I couldn't sleep. Must have been the bed.' She managed the suspicion of a smile, but her face was tear-stained.

'I was afraid I'd lost you.'

'I had to go with Kirsty.'

'I knew that.'

'Then I thought it will be all family. The awful journey ahead of us. Helping to rebuild everything. By that time I'll be so involved. And you wouldn't want to come back. Would you?'

'Any time.' He kissed her, gently at first. Their embrace became long and enthusiastic. 'We'll go back to the McDhuie territory whenever you want.'

'Darling Quentin. Do you know what I want now?'

'Something improbable.'

'Kippers for breakfast.' She put her hand in his pocket.

Together they turned towards the hotel.